We Decided On Forever

NIDA AHMED

KALAMOS LITERARY SERVICES

Kalamos Literary Services LLP
Email: kalamosliteraryservices@gmail.com
Published in 2017
by
Kalamos Literary Services
ISBN- 9789384315603

Price- 175 ₹

To my only loving Brother,
MOMIN SHEIKH *(late)*
I know you must be seeing me, making fun of me (like you always did)
and feeling proud of me from Heaven.

"Buss ek shaqs mere dil ki zidd hai,
na uss jaisa chahiye, na uske siwa chahiye."

31st December 2016
11:11 PM

Dear Diary,

They say wishes come true at this hour and I'd like to believe them. Because what I dream of is nothing short of a miracle. And for that, I have to believe in the power of magic.

And the greatest magic trick of all time is 'true love.' Right? After all it was true love's kiss that woke Sleeping Beauty up.

But how can one be sure that they are in 'love'?

In a world where commitment is a phobia and girls are a chase, how can one be sure that what they have is indeed love?

My friends say that there are "signs" that

prove that he loves you too. These might be making your days, as his special days, or being constantly in sync. Connected always.

Personally, I have never understood this definition. For how can one articulate the definition of a feeling? I find it easier to trust Blaise Pascal on this- "The heart has its reason which reason knows not!"

After all, however much we try or learn to be strong, we kneel before our heart. Because even after infinite failed attempts, one memory, one song, one moment is all it takes to make us weak from within.

Moreover, is it enough for two people to be in love for a "Happily Ever After?" This is something every fairy tale writer should ponder upon. Is every Prince Charming's mother going to welcome a commoner Cinderella to her splendid place?

I have always been someone who has chased logic in almost everything; but it is here that

I lose all my wit. Matters of heart, indeed, know no reason.

And I'll walk into another year not knowing what to make of my past year, my past mistakes, my past weaknesses, my past decisions. But I've decided that I'll be happy.

Happy about my life.

Happy about my decisions.

Happy about my achievements.

I'll live on my own terms, with my own beliefs; Only Khuda would be my judge.

#1 Home Coming

Umar is a major part of my small world. Though we are not related by blood, his presence in my life has always made me feel like I've got an elder brother to fall back on. Today, I can trust two men blindly- my father and Umar.

He hails from a business family, and had been in New York for the last 6 years to handle business. But the miles never added to the distance between our hearts. Fulfilling all my wishes and desires was his priority.

Like any brother, he could read me without me having to utter a word. He would then do the dirty work of taking care of my problems. I've always felt blessed to have him as my Guardian Angel. So, when I got the news that he is coming back from USA next week, my happiness knew no bounds.

Yet I was scared.
Scared of what I might say when he'd look me in the eyes and ask me how was I?
Did I have it in me to lie to him?
Would he notice the pain in my eyes and withdrawal in my voice?
And somehow, I knew the answers to all my questions.

He'd read me like an open book. And that, strangely, made me feel a little at peace. I knew it for a fact that he would never judge me. After all, it is Umar! My brother. I'll try my very best to hide my misery but when the day comes, I won't hold myself back. He'd be my witness and my advocate when the All Powerful decides our fate.

On Sunday, he came to our home for dinner. And his welcome was nothing short of a festival. All the love and attention was showered on him and I was thankful. That gave me an alibi and helped me prepare myself better. I wanted to be the same Alfisha, the one he left behind on the dusty roads of Delhi 6 years ago; the one he knew and understood well.

Umar's equation with my sister, My Appi, was another welcoming distraction. They just never seemed to get along. So, the conversation at the dinner table was mostly a sweet banter between Appi and Umar.

"Aren't your New York fancy friends missing your exuberant company, janab?" Appi inquired. Umar gave a smirk and replied "They might. But I missed your company and hence came back". "Maybe you've been declared an outcast. New Yorkers don't want you anymore. Right?" asked Appi. "Maybe, maybe not! You seemed to know a lot about me. Pray, enlighten everyone here why would that happen?" replied Umar. To this, Appi had a strange twinkle in her eye. However, all she said was "I would love to. I know you better than anyone on this dinner table. They seem oblivious to your fangs and tail. However, it is an Allah loving household and I'd rather not talk about the Shaitan here."

By now, I was thoroughly annoyed. It was supposed to be a nice dinner where everyone could spend quality time with Bhai. To make my thoughts clear, I went against my nature and yelled at them to be quiet and relish the food laid out in front of them.

Even to this my Appi had an observation to make- "Everything had to be what he loves to eat, of course!"

The naïve me could never understand why they would never get along. Anyhow, by now my mother was also seated and so the feast began!

After having the first byte of the food laid out on his plate, Umar complimented my mother. "Aunty I can never forget the taste of your delicious food. Especially this Biriyani." My mother took this compliment as another feather in her cap and thanked him. In the same breath, she added "Isn't Delhi too hot in summers? I would love to be at a cool place right now, where I won't sweat this much". Bhai agreed. His solution, however, was just as impractical as it can get. "Aunty lets shift to some cold, windy and chilled place," was his suggestion.

Maa didn't look very impressed on this. However, she masked her disappointment with "We should head to some hill station during the holidays." To this my Appi added, "He'd rather go to Agra. The asylum would suit him best."

Umar completely ignored Appi and got into a discussion with Maa. He suggested every famous hill station in north India, from Manali to Shimla, but my mother had the befitting reply of 'been there, done that.' However, both agreed on one place – Kashmir.

Even the mere mention of that place raised hair on my arms. I didn't want to be there. I couldn't go there. No! It is the reason for my misery. Is there no other place left to visit?

To avoid further discussion over that damned place I put forth a feeble plea. "The weather is changing and Delhi isn't all that bad," I said. And suddenly all pairs of eyes were on me. After a few seconds, Umar asked me if I was serious. Oh, how hard my heart wanted to yell that I was. But I didn't want him to know. Not yet. Not like this.

I tried to refute but failed miserably. So, I collected my freshly wounded self and decided to go and hide in my room so that I wouldn't have to explain myself.

It was there, in my small cosy room, that I started contemplating my life. And everything related to my past flashed in front of my eyes, just like it does in the movies.

Why is it that whenever anything remotely related to him is mentioned, I overreact? I could have easily said "No" to the idea of Kashmir visit, without sounding so rude.

More importantly, why couldn't I have control over my feelings even after two years? After all, time is supposed to heal everything. Then why couldn't it heal me? Why is it that I just learnt how to be normal yet never came back to who I used to be?

People say things change with time. Indeed! However, they never go back to what they used to be. Just like how at times I feel like I'm a mere shadow of who Alfisha earlier used to be. The truth is, feelings never change. We just learn to express them in a different way or learn to hide them. But no one can change them.

I know I was doing wrong to myself. Over thinking and overanalysing wouldn't help me.
I didn't deserve all this.
But what could I really do? The heart wants what it wants. Even if it can't have it.
I felt so helpless.

I didn't realize how and when my eyes got moist. Neither did I realise that Umar had entered my room and was looking at me with sorry eyes. "Are you going to tell me what is wrong with you?" I just shook my head in reply. Clearing my throat, I meekly said, "nothing". Not pressing the matter further, he inquired about my college and how did it feel like to be an adult. I replied to every question mechanically.

"What do you want to do after graduation, Alfisha?" This question caught my attention. "I want to do a MA, Bhai. I want to write. I want to be the voice of people who can't really express what they feel. I feel that every human being should be able to communicate, without holding themselves back. I want to understand and empathise over the reasons that hold us back from expressing what we feel. I want the world to be a place where we can talk and communicate freely. Till then, I'd keep sending my voice in the void. Maybe, someday, someone would read it and feel that they are not alone. That it is okay to go through what they are going through right now."

Umar looked at me, amazed. "Kid, you've grown up. It really has been a long time since we sat down and talked." I smiled a little. It felt good to know that I've grown. For better or for worse? That is open to interpretation of course.

"I've got a wedding to attend on Thursday, would you like to accompany me?" he asked as he made himself at ease and sat beside me, on my bed. He continued, "One of my friends can help you out with the idea of how to be a writer. He'd be pleased to meet you." Excitedly I said, "Yes, of course!" I felt so relieved to know that Bhai loved and supported my goals. Moreover, I'd get one step closer to achieving my dream. But my happiness was short-lived as I heard him say, he'll book our tickets to Pune.

"We'll be back by the weekend unless you want to visit someplace around Pune."

I couldn't breathe. Pune? But, why? Why couldn't the wedding be in Delhi or anywhere other than Kashmir or Pune?

"Answer me. Do you want to explore the city or not?" Bhai inquired. I mumbled something. And finally told him I couldn't go. He looked shocked. "But you said yes just a couple of minutes back. What changed in such a short span of time?". "I just remembered I have a submission due then, so I can't come. Sorry, Bhai."

My mind started to work at higher gears and suddenly my face turned red. Bhai had to shake me to bring me back to Earth.

"Don't you dare tell me you're okay. Tell me what is wrong. Right now, Alfisha!"

His tone shook me. I couldn't hold my tears back.

"He lives there Bhai. How can I go to Pune and not see him? I will not be able to resist. And what if he does not even recognize me? No. I can't. What if he has moved on? I can't see him with any other girl. No. I can't go there," I mumbled in between sobs.

"It's okay. We won't go" he said as he hugged me. "Now tell me, who lives there. And tell me everything, got it?" I nodded my head as I tried to collect myself.

"RAYAN," I said, feebly.

"…okay. And…?"

"I love him, Bhai. I really do. Even though I'm trying to live without him but it feels like he is around me, all the time, subconsciously. It's not in my control. I've tried to forget him. I don't want to miss him. I feel helpless, Bhai. I can't go to Pune. Please. He lives there. I can't," I said as I broke into another round of sobs.

"Alright, we're not going there. But you've got to tell me what is wrong, love? And don't hold back now. Please."

And so, I began with my life story.

#2 The Beginning of a Good Time

My doom began exactly two years ago, and it wasn't slow or gradual; but rather a sudden halt. In retrospect, I've come to realise that I've grown a lot, but there was a time when I was a zombie. Someone who wouldn't repose; but just carry on doing things.

…and all that can be traced back to one guy, over one summer that changed my life completely.

And for Umar to know all about that, I had to fish out my old journals. I knew that I might not do justice to my story. My emotions would get better of me, my heart would distract me and my words would betray me. He had the right to know everything. And I was done being strong.

He was my support system and I wanted him to know about my pain, my plight, my wait. I wanted him to know the new Alfisha. The one he couldn't understand.

15-08-10
9:00

Dear Diary,

Finally, I made my Facebook ID. It wasn't easy to get my father on board for this. But you know me, who can stop Alfisha when she sets her heart on something? And within a few hours, I got five friend requests. Didn't I tell you I am a hotshot!

However, I ignored all of them except one. Just for the fun of it I accepted the friend request of 'Dashing Smarty'. And our initial conversation was weird. It made me aware of our differences and brought us to the realization that we were poles apart from each other on every count and could never be friends.

So here is how the conversation went:

Me: Hey! Do I know you?

Him: No, but I really want to know you.

Me: Sorry! I don't talk to strangers.

Him: However, you accepted my friend request.

Me: Not every Facebook friend is someone you know, or want to know.

Him: So, that means you have accepted my request just to see my hot and sexy pics.

Me: Why not? After all you are the "Dashing Smarty!"

Him: My name is Rayan. And I really Liked your name, that why I sent you the request.

Me: Thanks.

Him: You're welcome

And that was the end of it.

Now I'm certain that the world is filled with strange people.

22-09-10

8:05

Dear Diary,

The graduation from fighting over trifles to being friends and then to best friends, has happened in a blink of an eye. My days don't see an end without hearing from him. I couldn't even wish for more. He always keeps me happy. At times, we laugh and there are times where I feel sad for not being able to see him. The fact is, I am from Delhi and he is from Kashmir. So meeting each other is not possible, yet.

Lately, we've started talking about our past and started discussing our future. The conversations get interesting, just like this one:

He: Do you have a boyfriend?

Me: Not really. :P

He: What does that mean?

Me: Well, I have a crush on one of my friend.

He: And... does he like you?

Me: I am confused.

He: Okay...

Me: What about you? Single?

He: No, I have a girlfriend and we are in a committed relationship.

Me: Oh! Good. There are very few people who are that loyal these days.

He: Yes. So, what all qualities do you want in your life partner?

Me: He should love me more than I love him.

He: That's all?

Me: Certainly.

He: That's quite...

Me: Quite what?

He: Impressive.

Me: What about you?

He: Oh, I have a very long list. She should be

intelligent, beautiful, caring and understanding and trustworthy.

Me: What do you mean by "should be"? You've already got a girlfriend.

He: Hmm.

Me: Then why is it "should" be? Or is she not whom you desire for?

He: Of course, she is.

Me: Good for you.

He: Hmm.

2-12-10
11:00

Dear Diary,

So, things are going fine on the Rehan front. I think I am attracted towards him more than I pay heed to it. And today I got down to thinking as to why I'm so drawn to him.

He looks elegant and impressive. Moreover, we've grown up together. Our parents are close friends. He is different from others and

I like that distinct trait about him. He is me from the other gender. In every function or get together, our eyes look for each other. His presence fires me with enthusiasm. His source of envy is every other guy in the society who I talk with. I always believed that whosoever will come in my life, should be like me.

We see each other every day and smile, and always try to talk and know each other better.

Rehan was the closest thing I had to a "crush."

And for a young, hormonal teenage girl, that was something to be thrilled about. More so because my friends were convinced that I've sworn myself off of guys. To know that I had a crush was of extreme importance; to them more than me.

However, Rayan never took it in the same spirit. According to him, Rehan might be a nice guy but he could never be good enough for me.

12-1-11
7:10

Dear Diary,

It's over.

Rehan and I are done.

Once he messaged me and from that day we started talking. After talking to him I realized, may be our habits and likes match, but both of us are different from each other. Our nature was quite different and even after trying much to know and understand each other, we had failed. And maybe the feelings were mutual.

We both decided to continue as friends and never took this friendship any further.

I'll always want him to be happy even if it makes me sad in the process. I will always smile when someone mentions his name, or I see a picture of him, even if it also makes me a little bitter. Oh, yes I am over him. But I still care about him.

Looking back, I realize how time teaches us to differentiate between infatuation and genuine attraction. Rehan had every quality that I would look for in any guy but even that was not enough for me to stay with him.

Blame it on the young mind or prudish heart but you always look for that one 'wow' moment. That never came with Rehan. I got a smile every time Rayan texted; I don't know if I can say the same about Rehan.

Rehan was the perfect guy, but in a short span of time I understood that he wasn't my perfect guy.

Meanwhile, Rayan and I continued to talk daily. And one day I decided it was time for Appi to know about him.

16-02-11
8:00

Dear Diary,

It is rightly said that people with similar nature make great friends in no time. My sister and Rayan were similar in nature to a certain extent. The way they perceived the world was something I can never learn and can never understand. Both of them are chronic over-thinkers. Talking to people was something that did not come easily to them. They are the introverts, the creative types, the geniuses who get stimulation from learning rather than socializing. It's always the quiet ones who turn out to be the most interesting and surprising. Isn't it? Both held a very reserved personality. By looking at them, one cannot make out what they are thinking in their minds. Being hard-hearted and unsympathetic was something they were comfortable being. Both had a hidden ability to build walls around their hearts that prevented them from being in tune with the emotions that would lead them towards happiness and positive changes in their lives. It is not that they do not think with their hearts, but the ultimate decision would always be from the mind.

On the other hand, I have always been a

dreamer, an admirer of beauty. Life has always been hunky dory for me. I am somebody who always looks for magic in the world. As per me, the world is a place animated with living things, where every rock possesses invisible eyes and a certain joie de vivre.

Rayan and Appi, however, are more attuned to practicality and common sense. They see less mystery in the world, and to me they are more of a strange creature, always seeking to simplify the inexplicable to what can be explained.

But maybe, we all are wrong in possessing these traits of dreaming and practicality. My experiences in life have taught me that a person should not be so practical that he fears dreaming, and a person should not be such a dreamer either that he loses his sight of reality to the shine of positivity in the world.

The fact is Appi's friends know me very well

so I wanted Appi to know Rayan as well.

I wanted her to know, how close Rayan and I were. I knew, that this Facebook friendship; being close even without meeting once; all this was something my sister wouldn't trust and would never approve of. But somewhere deep down in my heart I knew this bond would last a lifetime.

So, today I introduced Rayan to Appi. As expected, Appi's first sentence after speaking to him was "bahut kam bolta hai" (he does not talk much). They didn't chat much but were able to read each other's nature. Appi was the first person, who made me look at Rayan's positive individuality and his affectionate character, traits that I could not imagine existed in him. In fact, Appi has now become one of the biggest fans of Rayan's voice and his songs.

Before talking to her, Rayan was shy and fearsome of Appi. That may be because I portrayed her as such. He was very aware of the fact that Appi was older to him and without her advices and mature suggestions; my parents would not do anything.

26-02-11
6:05

Dear Diary,

I was at my khaala's place when Rayan called. He went on to tell me that Naushaali and him have broken up. I was surprised to listen to this at that time because I had always thought he wasn't one of those men who play with girls and their feelings. So I've decided that from now on I will stay distant from him.

And now he has a new girlfriend that he wants me to talk to. Should I? I mean yes, we are close but what would she think? I really don't want to be in the middle of a nasty conversation. Perhaps, I'll just say Hi and that'll be all.

We'll see.

27-02-11

7:15

Dear Diary,

Could it be something more that is brewing between Rayan and me? I mean today's conversation made me rethink about our dynamics. However, it's his 12th standard and I'm not going to ruin anything for him because of what I might think exists between the two of us.

He: Hey! You remember you have to talk to my girlfriend today, right?

Me: Hahaha! Yes, put her on the call

He: Alright, Hold on.

Tanzeel: Hey Alfisha! Tanzeel here. How are you?

Me: I am good and what about you?

Tanzeel: I am good.

He: Alfisha see she doesn't let me call you my Jaan (darling/ love/ honey).

Tanzeel: Because there can only be one jaan.

Me: Agreed.

He: Why are you kidding?

Me: Can you shut up for a while?

Tanzeel: Hmm.

Me: So, Tanzeel how does it feel to be in a relationship?

Tanzeel: It feels great! Loving someone so dearly, caring for that person, knowing his likes and dislikes is an altogether new experience and I love it.

Me: Oh. Sounds so good. So you know his likes and dislikes?

Tanzeel: Yes.

He: Are you sure?

Tanzeel: What do you mean? Of course, I am sure.

He: So, may I ask you some questions right now?

Me: Can I go?

Tanzeel: It's fine. Bring it on.

He: What's my favourite dish?

Tanzeel: Chicken?

He: Alfisha?

Me: I think it's paneer.

He: Paneer it is.

Tanzeel: Is it? I'll try to remember it from now on.

He: Okay, who is my favourite actor?

Tanzeel: Shahrukh Khan?

He: Alfisha?

Me: "Khud ko hero se kam nahi samajhta ye."

He: My weakness?

Me: Not good at expressing your feelings.

Tanzeel: You guys continue. My mom is calling. I have to go.

He: Okay bye.

Me: No Tanzeel... wait! I am the one who should leave. See. Rayan and me are just good friends. We just know each other too well. That's all.

Tanzeel: Hmmm.

He: She knows that. You don't need to give explanation.

* Tanzeel disconnected*

Me: Uffff...Rayan are you sick?

He: What's wrong?

Me: She is your girlfriend Rayan. She has the right to know you. And it was wrong on your part to give me more importance than what she should be given.

He: It's not my fault if you know me more than she does.

Me: Hmm.

He: Don't worry about her. I will take care

of that.

Me: Hmmm.

He: By the way ... My god. You really know everything about me.

Me: I know I am great.

> **Call disconnected**

- Year Summary

It had now been about a year and a half since we had known each other.

This year was a crucial year for Rayan, he had his 12th boards. Therefore, we didn't talk much this year. I always prayed for him. I guess I never realized it, but his happiness was always important to me, as it is even now.

Maashah Allah! He scored 86 percent marks and went to Pune to study further. He wanted to pursue BA LLB. Call it his fortune, the impact of my prayers or the reservation for Kashmiri migrants, he got into one of the best law colleges in Pune, BVP.

#3 Retrospection

Rayan and I used to talk for almost 24 hours in a day, seven days a week. I used to care for even the slightest of his whims and fancies. I had realized that he was alone in Pune. He had to manage his life and his daily chores on his own, be it cooking or washing dishes and clothes, or fetching water. I still remember I used to come back from my *daadu's* place early on *Eid* so that I could speak to Rayan on the phone. I knew he would be terribly missing his family on *Eid* but wouldn't acknowledge it. But with me he didn't need to specifically mention things, or talk about them; I understood. And somewhere deep down even he knew that I won't leave him alone; I'll come back early so that I could speak to him.

About two three months later, sometime in August, Rayan messaged me saying he nearly escaped death today, as there was a bomb blast nearby that had injured many. That was the first time I cried for Rayan. I was paranoid, calling him every hour to check on him. It was then that I realized that I love him.

He sang for me the first time that day. I had no idea he could sing that well!

He: *Dil ko tumse pyaar hua… pehli baar hua…*

Tumse pyaar hua...

Mai bhi aashiq yaar hua... pehli baar hua

Tumse pyaar hua

Chahe hai... betaabi... meri jaan...

kaho mai kya karu-2

dil ko tumse pyaar hua... pehli baar hua

Tumse baar hua

Me: Ravz, I love it!

He: What is Ravz?

Me: Your new nickname.

He: Why Ravz?

Me: Because, I love this name.

He: Okay, *Bulbul.*

Me: *Bulbul?*

He: Yes, now you are my *Bulbul.*

Me: …okay.

Ravz… this was a name I read in Ravindra Singh's novel, "Can Love Happen Twice?" and since then this name has been close to me. I had always thought that whenever someone special will become a part of my life, I will call him Ravz. *Allah* knows why I uttered this name for him, but it happened so naturally, on its own accord. We talked throughout the day; we couldn't survive without speaking to each other over the phone.

Almost one year later when he confessed his love for me, I rejected. Somehow, I could never tell him that I loved him too. Probably because I knew that even if we wanted it, we have no future together. He was from Kashmir, while I was from Delhi. I had no brother; there was just one elder sister. How could I leave my parents and go to a new place where I knew nobody? And even he couldn't leave his parents. I guess it was only right to reject his proposal at that time, and that is what I did.

After this, he gave up on me and I gave up on us. Our conversations started decreasing. We even started ignoring each other over phone and subscribed to the easy lie- 'Sorry, I was busy.'

It took one incident, one tragic mishap that brought back my friend, the one I held close to my heart. The one who could mend me like no one.

5-05-11
3:30

Dear Diary,

Today maamu called and informed that nani's health was critical. By the time I could comprehend what he said; he called back and said that she passed away.

My nani's demise was a shock to me. I was very close to her, and her death felt like the end of the world to me. Rayan's exams are going on and we have decided that we won't speak to each other till the time he gets done with his exams. And so, I won't call him.

All I want to do is cry my heart out and feel at peace. But how can I do that? When the most special piece of my heart is gone and has now left a permanent void in my life. One that no one else can fill.

25-05-11
11:00

Dear Diary,

I informed Rayan about nani's inteqaal (demise) today (twenty days later).

The conversation ended up something like this.

Me: Rayan naani passed away.

He: When? How? Why didn't you tell me?

Me: 5th of May. Your exams were going on,

that's why I didn't bother you.

He: Baby, am I the last one to know about this?

Me: Hmm.

He: Is everyone at home fine?

Me: Recovering. It'll take time.

He: And you? Are you okay?

Me: I don't know. I would be...eventually.

He: You must be. You are very strong, Jaan. You are the source of my strength and belief. Now you need to be the Jaan of your family. Everybody in your family expects you to change the atmosphere. To make everybody laugh. More importantly, I want to see you laugh.

Me: I know. But even I need someone to listen to me. I want to cry hard. I want someone to hold me tight, hug me and tell me that it'll be alright.

He: It would work out great, love.

Me: Hmm.

He: You were the closest to her, I know. But you need to understand that she is in a better place now.

Me: Yes.

He: You know why she loved you so dearly?

Me: *silence*

He: Because you are just like her. You can't see anyone cry; nor can you hurt anyone. Jaan, you are as sweet as she was. She saw herself in you. And I see her through you.

Me: I can't be like her, Ravz. NEVER.

He: You are. More than you can realize. Right now, you have to act strong; support your family.

 And please remember one very important thing.

Me: What?

He: That I Love You.

Me: Jee.

To be honest, I have stopped asking for anything from Allah, I just thank him for giving me that one person I had always asked for in my prayers. I now feel that I don't need anything else from this world, because Allah has bestowed me with the most beautiful thing on this planet "Rayan". His most beautiful creation -Ravz.

#4 About the spoken love

For this one conversation, I don't need to go back to my beloved diaries.

It feels like yesterday that it happened and it still brings out the blush on my cheeks. It might sound naïve now. The world has moved on at a very fast pace but for an old school person like me, it took a lot of effort and thought to say the three most underrated words. Those, which had the power to move mountains and be eternal. The ones, I believe, are the true ibadat of Allah.

He: I love you.

Me: I love you too.

He: Are you serious?

Me: When have I lied to you?

He: That's not the point. Do you really love me?

Me: Yes.

He: How much?

Me: More than you do.

He: My God, dreams do come true. You have no clue what this means to me.

 I can't express my feeling right now.

YOU love ME.

Now, I can share everything with you.

Me: But, you always share everything with me.

He: Not exactly. I am talking about all the dirty stuff which keeps going in my mind

whenever I see your pics. Like you have no idea how cute you are. And the way you say "HELLO".

Hayeeeee!

Me: Hahaha, relax Ravz.

He: I can't.

Me: Why are you laughing so much?

He: I am not laughing. I am Happy.

Very Happy!

Me: …okay.

He: So, do you love me more than I do?

Me: YES.

He: Then why didn't you ever say it?

Me: Because I was scared.

He: Scared of what?

Me: Of attachments and expectations. And what the future holds for us. I don't want this to be just another fling. I want this to mean something. My idea is to grow in love with you, and not just falling in it. If I'm in this, it'll be forever.

He: *Jaan,* I love you! And I promise we will always be together. It's not just you. *We have decided on forever.* Together.

Me: Rayan you need to understand that forever is a long time and our journey won't be an easy one. You've admitted that your mom always wanted a Kashmiri girl as her daughter-in-law, someone who could speak in Kashmiri, cook Kashmiri food. They'll never accept me.

He: *Jaan,* I've already told mom that I'll marry the girl I love. So, don't worry, everything will be fine.

Me: …it's not the same.

He: Do you trust me?

Me: Yes, I do.

He: Then don't worry.

Me: Okay

He: *Muaaah*

Since that day, I had started considering myself '*Allah's*' beloved child, who was always being looked upon by Him. After my father, it was Ravz whom I trusted. He was probably not even aware that he had filled my life with magic.

I understood we had to face a lot of problems before we could finally be together but I had a firm belief that everything would be fine and when the time would come, courage would make its way.

I'm sure people wonder; can somebody fall in love with someone else, so deeply, without even seeing them ever? And in my opinion, it is a yes. He loved me and I loved him, beyond a cognizable . We loved each other deeply, madly, irrevocably.

And distance and situations were not going to change that.

5 Broken Promises

By 2013, Ravz and I had completed three years together and we firmly believed that we were made for each other. In these three years, we stood by each other through all ups and downs, through everything happy and sad, and we started dreaming that the way these three years were spent in mirth, the rest of our lives would be as such. Such was my love for him that his name preceded mine, in all our prayers.

But I guess I should have warded off the evil's eye from my happiness. *'Allah'* knows better whose evil eye took away my happiness.

Rayan's behaviour towards me drastically transformed, all of a sudden. I had no clue as to what I was supposed to do, if anything at all.

12-16-13
7:30

Dear Diary,

I feel something is off. Something is wrong and he won't tell me about it.

So today, I decided I'd cut to the chase and ask him what I had done to displease him. Why had he suddenly started to ignore me.

It started from a phone call two days back.

Me: Hey!

He: Hi.

Me: How are you?

He: Good, what about you?

Me: Fine.

He: Hmm.

Me: Are you fine, really?

He: Yes, I am good.

Me: Can we talk right now?

He: No, I am busy.

Me: Okay, I'll call you in the evening.

He: No, please don't.

Me: Why?

He: I need to go somewhere else.

Me: Oh okay, no problem.

He: Hmm. I'll talk to you later.

Me: Okay, bye.

IN THE EVENING (on text)

Me: There?

He: Yes.

Me: ...Could've dropped a text...

He: I told you I was busy; don't you get it?

Me: You've been busy all this while?

He: Yes, so?

Me: Ravz... Is everything fine?

He: Yes!

Me: Okay.

He: Hmm... let's talk tomorrow.

Me: Okay bye.

He: Bye.

By now I've understood that "hmm," the one word Ravz loved; held the key to his heart. His 'Hmm' meant yes, and it hid what he truly felt. He doesn't know how to express his feelings or speak about out, but I can understand everything. I knew there was something troubling him which he wasn't telling me, because he knew that it would hurt me.

Today, when I called I was adamant to know what his "hmm" meant.

He: Hey! Had your meals?

Me: No.

He: Why?

Me: First answer my question.

He: Yes, ask.

Me: Ravz, you know I love you, right?

He: Yes, jaan and I love you too!

Me: You know that I trust you the most?

He: Yes, I do.

Me: Then you must also know that you can't hide anything from me even if you try hard to.

He: Hmm.

Me: Now tell me what is wrong, please.

He: Baby, I love you. More than anyone. More than anything, that is why I told everybody at my home about you and about us, and my mom outright rejected you. She said the girl must be Kashmiri and cannot be from Delhi, come what may.

Me: What?

He: Yes, I tried hard to make them understand, I tried a lot, but they are just not ready to accept you.

Me: I told you this would happen but you said you'd take care of it. Why don't you?

He: What else do I do now? I thought if I keep trying for some time, things will get alright, but my parents are just not ready to understand.

Me: But Ravz you said that you have already told your parents that you will marry the girl of your choice and they will not have a problem.

He: Yes, they are saying choose any Kashmiri girl, but it cannot be a girl from Delhi.

Me: Why? What is so wrong in marrying a Delhi girl? I am just as normal as any Kashmiri girl.

He: I don't know.

Me: What do you mean by you don't know?

He: I am trying. I don't have any idea what are they thinking.

Me: So now?

He: Now what?

Me: Ravz, this is a deal breaker for me and you know that. We decided on forever.

He: I have tried my level best. Now tell me what else do I do?

Me: What is their problem with me?

He: Just that you are not a Kashmiri.

Me: That's it?

He: Hmm.

Me: So, I will learn Kashmiri. Would that make me a suitable choice?

He: That won't make any difference.

Me: Excuse me?

He: You have no idea what all I am going through. You are fighting with me and I am fighting with my parents for you. And the sad part is both of you are accusing me for no reason.

Me: ...I am just worried.

He: And I am not? Right?

Me: ...

He: Everything will be fine INSHAALLAH.

Me: IN SHA ALLAH.

He: hmm... Sleep now, it's too late. We'll talk tomorrow morning.

Me: Okay bye.

He: Bye

But sleep didn't come to me that night. What else could I have done to make his parents feel that way? The entire night I kept thinking was it just because I am from Delhi that Ravz's parents had rejected me, or is it something else?

Everybody's parents love them with all their heart and the only dream parents live with is to see their child happy. Was this not enough for Ravz's parents that he loved me and I was the centre of all his happiness?

Like every girl even I dream of a man who loves me dearly. Laughing, being chirpy and loving is an indispensable part of my personality and probably that is why people said that I can win people's hearts. Now the only thing I wish for was Allah to give me one chance to meet Ravz's parents and I would put in my heart and soul to win them over.

The only problem they had with me was that I was from Delhi? So, for them I'll learn to speak in Kashmiri, learn to cook Kashmiri food, their rituals...everything. I won't give them even one chance to complain about me.

I know how much his family means to Ravz. I know the day Ravz's parents accept me; there would be no turning back. Here I am, planning to spend my entire future with him, and on the other side I don't even know what he is thinking.

4-07-13

9:30

Dear Diary,

Things are not the same. The love is still there but the dynamic is lost. There was a certain sort of inhibition in sharing our emotions and feelings with each other, probably because a major complication had come up which would not let us be together and this was somehow scary to both of us.

But it was today that I realized that the boat I had pinned my hopes on for my survival had already drowned; taking me down with him.

He: Hi

Me: Hey! Where have you been? Your phone was busy all this while.

He: I was talking to someone.

Me: To whom?

He: Vartika.

Me: Who is she?

He: A friend.

Me: So, you've been talking to her for the past one hour?

He: Yeah...so?

Me: Okay.

He: Hmm.

Me: Any plans for tomorrow?

He: Oh! Yes, I am going out with Vartika tomorrow.

Me: What?!

He: Why are you surprised?

Me: Ravz is Vartika your girlfriend?

He: Hmm

Me: What hmm? Speak out!

He: Yes, she is.

Me: Are you serious?

He: Yes, I am serious. She is my girlfriend and now we should maintain a certain distance because the reality is that we can't ever be together now.

Me: Ravz, we can always find a solution, right? At least we can try?

He: There are no solutions to some problems.

Me: Then...

He: Then...move on, what else?

Me: Are you happy with her?

He: I will be.

Me: Okay, then stick to her.

He: And what about you?

Me: You do what you want to do and I'll do what I want to.

He: Okay.

Me: Bye.

He: Bye.

Even to this day I am left wondering, how can a person undergo such a drastic change suddenly?

Was I never important in his life? He didn't even wait for me to go and my place was already given to somebody else.

How could he?

Is it so easy?

First you fall in love with someone, make them believe that you love them. Then make promises to them, transform their lives and make them dream with open eyes. When things get tough, apologize and quote some excuse for not being together. And then say "move on in life."

And if it was so easy, why couldn't do it?

Am I so weak? So feeble?

I know I wasn't earlier, but now I am not too sure.

Ravz had become my biggest weakness. When? Why? How? Even I didn't realize. I knew one thing and that was if I stay with him any longer, I'd be hurt. More than I could handle; more than I could imagine.

Despite knowing all of this, I couldn't resist talking to him. I just couldn't stop myself.

While he was spending most of his time with

Vartika, I spent mine thinking about him.

I guess this is what they call love, wanting to see the other happy in every circumstance, even if his happiness lies in somebody else's and not yours.

I was tolerating all of this because he was happy and Vartika was a nice girl. He hoped that someday I too would fall for someone.

10-08-13
8:25

Dear Diary,

It pains my heart to see that he is happy with someone else. If he really loved me, would he put me through this hell? Is this what I deserve for loving him with all that I have? With all my being?

He sends me her photographs. He tells me how adorable she is. The other day, he sent me a picture of a huge teddy bear and a birthday card that were meant to be her birthday gift.

I can't explain what I'm experiencing; it is a

mix of pain, hurt and restlessness. And sure, it doesn't feel nice. I can see my dreams shattering in front of my eyes and it is my beloved who is plunging daggers into my heart; while I witness my doom as a mute spectator.

I have lost faith in myself so much that at one point I felt like putting an end to myself was the solution to my misery. But is it? Is he worth that? While tears flow down my check, almost daily, did he even bother to ask if I was okay?

Is this the end of my happily ever after? Have I fallen for the wrong guy? Did he ever even love me at all? Was our forever just in words?

These questions haunt me every day. He is all I think of, consciously and subconsciously. To the world, I seem lost. To myself, I seem broken. Earlier it was just emotionally, yesterday I added physically to the list as well.

I missed a step and fell down a flight of stairs. What was I thinking? I was dreaming about Rayan coming back to me, telling me that he loves me and we'd be happy again; like we were before.

It had been two days since I hadn't been online. So with my foot wrapped in bandages, I logged in my FB account, only to find Rayan's messages in my inbox. I didn't reply.

Maybe, he saw that I was online because the very next minute he sent another message.

He: ?

Me: Jee?

He: Where were you? All these days and not a single text?

Me: I fell down from the staircase.

He: What? How? Why didn't you tell me?

Me: Just fell off.

He: How many injuries? The injuries aren't

very serious, are they?

Me: A couple of bruises here and a couple of cuts there. Other than that, I'm fine.

He: Are you insane? Can't you take care of yourself?

Me: Calm down, I am fine.

He: Tell me everything.

Me: What do you mean by 'everything'? It's none of your business.

He: Show me where you are hurt.

Me: No.

He: Why?

Me: Because, that's none of your concern.

He: Stop being such a brat, Alfisha.

Me: I'm just trying to move on. I have people around who can take care of me.

He: How hard is it for you to understand that I can't see you like this?

Me: What happened to you? I thought you had moved on?

He: Moved on? That can never happen. You rule my heart. I really love you a lot, Jaan.

Me: What about Vartika?

He: I was just trying to divert my mind, my emotions. I thought if I will ignore you and spend time with some other girl, go out with her, talk to her, I'll be able to forget you, but I failed. And miserably so.

Me: And you didn't even care about what I would go through? How would I feel?

He: I was doing all of this for you only. Allah forbid, if tomorrow we aren't together what would happen to you? Think about it once! I am a man; I will still find some way out, but what about you?

Me: Ravz, I can't predict the future and neither can you. Does that mean we have to live in the shadows of what could've been? Why can't we just live one day at a time?

We're still young. Too young in fact to be worrying about all this. If we stay together like this, till the end, they will have to agree.

He: And what if they don't agree?

Me: Please don't be such a pessimist, just pray to 'Allah' and everything would be fine.

He: Are you sure?

Me: Hmm… You love me, right?

He: Very much.

Me: Then I am sure.

Perhaps, my accident was the shock that snapped him out of his shell. I have found my Ravz back; I couldn't even ask Allah for anything else.

3-12-13
7:30

Dear Diary,

The naïve brain wanders to all meadows that seem green and my mind always wandered to the backyard of Rayan's house in Kashmir. I always imagined how it would be different from Delhi.

 Things would be so different then. I'd have to learn Kashmiri, understand their culture, customs and faith. And with Rayan by my side, I feel like I could do all of it.

There is just one thing that really frightened me. What if my parents didn't allow me to go there?

I was the youngest in my house, everyone's darling. My dad didn't even let me go anywhere far for a trip alone, would he ever let me go to Kashmir? I have no brother; it's just me and my sister who are our parents' sole support. When the time comes, would my conscience allow me to leave them alone?

But today I saw a silver lining. If I couldn't got here, maybe he could.

Me: Ravz, what are your plans after doing BBA LLB?

He: Business.

Me: Why not LLM?

He: For that, I'd have to come to Delhi.

Me: Are you serious, Ravz?

He: Yes, indeed.

Me: You have no clue how excited I am right now.

He: Hahaha...either Delhi or I'll work somewhere abroad.

Me: Oh! Like?

He: New York may be.

Me: That's great. You have decent plans, they will be well executed. Insha Allah!

He: 'In Sha Allah' – write it like this.

Me: Okay, In Sha Allah

6 Of Betraying friends
and other things

Anjali, Inha and I were from different streams but had been together since day one. Due to 12th standard and being from different streams, we hardly got any time to spend together, but thankfully by *Allah's* grace that never affected our friendship.

Our friendship was the talk of our school. We trusted each other and stood by the correct decision, whether it was acceptable or not. Probably that is the reason why we had been together for so long.

Inha was the girl who was closest to my heart. She stood by me since childhood, my best friend. I had a previous Facebook account which I had given to Inha and I had created a new account for my own use. All her internet related work was usually done by me. One day she said that I was very lucky to have Rayan in my life. It used to make me very happy because somewhere deep down even I felt that *Allah Ta'la* dearly loves me and even he wants me to have all the happiness in this world.

Inha was a science student, and because we were in 12th standard, Inha had started taking coaching classes. She did not need any aid in her studies as she was very intelligent, but she was planning to appear for the MBBS exams. Hence everyone advised her to take coaching and not risk it.

It had been about two months since she joined the classes when she started liking a guy in her coaching class, whose name was Karan. We checked Karan's Facebook profile after she had told us about him. He was a smart guy with an impressive personality but his persona was that of a Casanova. I felt that he wasn't good enough for my Inha.

Every free period in school, Inha used to talk about him, what he said and how she reacted. I got tired after a point trying to explain to her that he must be saying all of this to every other girl.

There wasn't anything new about this but Inha was just not ready to understand.

Inha: You know what? I think that he likes me.

Me: It's nothing like that, just because he shared a laugh or two, doesn't mean he likes you.

Anjali: Yes, exactly. And Inha please focus on your studies for now. Getting into a reputed college should be your aim right now.

Me: I agree.

Inha: Guys, what is wrong with you? I am not building this up. I'm sure that it is not a one sided love affair.

Me: Okay, let's assume that what you stated is true. What are you going to do about it? You know your family better, don't you? Do you want me to list down the consequence?

Anjali: Yes. Even if he likes you, you know how your family would react. Especially when they find out that you're hanging out with a Hindu guy.

Inha: Guys, religion? Seriously?

Anjali: What?

Me: Of course! Don't get any ideas. Please. You

don't even know him!

Inha: You don't need to boast about how perfect you and Rayan are.

Anjali: *Abe oye,* stop talking nonsense, understood?

Me: …we'll come to your coaching tomorrow, and we'll meet him. Alright?

Inha: Done

Anjali: Done

16-06-14
8:30

Dear Diary,

Today was THE day when I met Inha's Karan. Sadly, what she projects and who he is are two drastically different versions of the same person.

When we went to Inha's coaching and met all her friends, including Karan, he gave a vibe that Inha was a time pass for him.

Till now, I have helped Inha make all the

decisions. I didn't want to give her wrong advice this time as well. So, I spent some time with Karan. I didn't like his cocky behaviour//.

It was later when I went home that I understood how right my intuition was about him. He had left a Facebook message for me.

Karan: ...Hey You! I think I like you.

Me: Lol :') Aren't you too paced up? Till yesterday it was my best friend, today you are trying it on me. Wah! Wah!

Karan: I know you are her best friend, but no girl would let go of a guy this rich and smart, right?

Me: Such smugness, much wow!

Karan: Hahaha. Good sense of humour. The fact remains that a lot of girls love me.

Me: Love? You accepted that the only reason girls go crazy for you is because you are rich.

Karan: Hmm. Point. But Inha loves me.

Me: You wish.

Karan: Now you will send her the screenshots of all of this to Inha, right?

Me: You bet.

And then I blocked him.

I don't know why my best friend had to fall for someone like him. Someone who never deserved her.

I knew that she would never take my word for this so I asked Rayan to talk to her. Later in the evening I got a text from Inha informing me how Rayan made her understand the situation and she believed my stand.

I feel so blessed right now. My love, my best friends, and everyone around me is finally happy and on the right track.

Looking back, I feel so naïve to have believed that Inha would've given up on Karan so easily. After all, I would've never done so if Rayan was questioned for the same. Meanwhile, Rayan and I had a fight again. His sister couldn't convince their parents to let him date me and so he went in that dark zone of ignoring me and my existence. At that point, I got frustrated. Didn't we have the same discussion last month? In fact, every month. Why couldn't he live in the present is something I wonder about. Every single day.

During those days of being upset and not talking, Rayan dropped a text that read "Block Inha and don't talk to her again." I couldn't make a head or tail of what he wrote. It was later, when he sent me the screenshots of their chats that I understood what was going on.

Inha had started texting Rayan after the Karan episode.

Inha: Hey!

Ravz: Heya!

Inha: How are you?

Ravz: Good, wbu?

Inha: I am good too

Ravz: That's great!

Inha: How is your girlfriend?

Ravz: Hahaha, she is you best friend as well. Don't you know how she is?

Inha: No, she doesn't talk much to anybody these days, she just stays very irritated. And you stay so cool; the two of you don't quite get along together, right?

Ravz: Hahaha she is just stressed because of the results. Our couple would always be A1.

Inha: Oh! Really... But what use, you two will never really end up together. Alfisha's dad will never send her to Kashmir and you will never come to Delhi.

Ravz: Be positive please, we will find an alternative.

Inha: There's no alternative. Don't you think it's better for the two of you to end everything?

Ravz: Why are you being so pessimistic?

Inha: I am telling you the truth! I know Alfisha and her family well, she won't accept this, but even she knows that you guys have no future.

Ravz: What Rubbish? She will try her 100% I

know she will never give up. I am sure of us.

Inha: Even I am sure that she will never leave her family. You can very well ask her.

Ravz: Yes, I will.

Inha: Tomorrow?

Ravz: No… tomorrow her result will be out.

Inha: So, what? If you really want her in your life don't delay it any further, ask her tomorrow.

Ravz: Hmmm.

AFTER OUR FIGHT

Inha: Did you ask her?

Ravz: Yes

Inha: And you got the same answer as I said you would?

Ravz: Hmm.

Inha: Now what?

Ravz: I have blocked her.

Inha: Oh! That's great!

Ravz: What?

Inha: I mean now you both will be able to move on… And believe me you deserve a better girl.

Ravz: I will talk to you later man, bye.

Inha: Okay, bye.

AFTER TWO DAYS

Ravz: Dude I have lost my love, even though I really love her man.

Inha: Hmm… do one thing; delete all her pictures from your cell phone. It will help you forget her.

Ravz: No, I can't do that. Sorry.

Inha: Do it man, don't you want to move on?

Ravz: No, I don't.

Inha: Don't be emotional, Rayan.

While reading these conversations, I felt as if I was reading my worst enemy's conversations; I couldn't believe it in wildest of my dreams that she was the same girl whom I treated like my own sister. But why was she doing all of this? What wrong had I done to her to deserve this treatment from her?

I got my answers as soon as I read the conversations further

Inha: I need to confess something.

Ravz: Yes say.

Inha: All that happened in the past few weeks was intentionally done by me; I wanted you and Alfisha to fight. I wanted the two of you to stop talking and that is why I forced you to ask her all those things on the day of her board results so that her happiest day turns into the worst. I also realised that you respected me and hence won't deny if I ask you to do so.

I mean I do all the hard work, I study more than her and then she scores more than me in the board exams! Not mine, but her parents would be called in the school.

I am more beautiful than her but still she has more friends than me, people love her more than me, they trust her more than me. But why? Why?

The person I used to meet daily, the person I loved, she stole him as well.

All of this was inside me since always, I kept tolerating but now I couldn't see all of this anymore. I couldn't tolerate any further.

Today she is alone and I am with you, to say the truth I am in extreme peace today.

Ravz: Inha, you should be ashamed of yourself. And now I will make sure that she never talks to you. Bye.

BLOCKED

And the saddest part was Inha converted my happy day into my worst. I worked hard, very hard to score 94 percent in my 12th standard. And the one person I wanted to share that with, fought with me on a petty issue. I could forgive Rayan but Inha? How could I?

She blamed me for what happened in her life. But what wrong did I do? Was it my fault that people were drawn to me? Was it my fault that Karan was a creep? Or was having Rayan by my side my only fault?

She blamed me for trying to take Karan away. And she thought that she would try to take Rayan away from me. Maybe it was my fault that I tried to protect her from Karan's true nature. Had I let her fall and come back to me later, she would've not acted this way.

Jealousy…it has a way of killing everything: interests, relations and people.

…And to think that she was my best friend.

The only good that came out of this was that I felt closer to Rayan. Our decision of forever had not just been my infatuation. Even in our fights, he'd look out for me. And the fact that I got into Hindu College after my counseling.

#7 Of plans and happy days

Trust is an emotion which strengthens every relationship. They say love isn't true if there is no trust in it and long distance relationships can survive only on the lines of trust. And I always considered myself too lucky that I had immense trust on my love.

My dominating extrovert nature made me write Ravz a long speech and he used to reply to it in two lines; maximum. Whenever I inquired if it was only I who had to do all the talking, with utmost love he would reply, "If you won't talk, who else would?"

The most surprising fact is that people who spent days, months and years together; in each other's arms, couldn't trust each other. But I could trust

Rayan with my life.

Those days, we used to plan a lot. About anything and everything.

22-08-14

9:00

Dear Diary,

I'm so excited.

So very excited.

He is coming to meet me.

Finally.

He just confirmed it. It was something like:

He: Guess, what?

Me: What?

He: I am coming to Delhi.

Me: When? How? I mean how suddenly?

He: No. I'll be there in January, maybe 21st

or 22nd January, on my way back from Kashmir to Pune

Me: OMG! Are you serious?

He: Yes, I am serious.

Me: When would you be going to Kashmir?

He: In November, perhaps.

Me: Allah's grace! finally after three and a half years we are finally meeting.

He: Yes, finally!

Me: Would you believe me if I tell you that I am dancing right now?

He: I have been dancing for the past ten minutes.

Me: We'll have so much fun, Ravz.

He: Yes, and I want to see you in a black frock.

Me: Yes sir, as you command.

He: Yes... and then second day jeans and a skirt on the third day and shorts on the fourth and then...

Me: Mister, please control yourself. You were coming for just two or three days, where did the fourth day come from?

He: ...I got a little carried away.

Me: Hehehe, you'll go back after a week. That's it, full and final. We're meeting after so long, at least we should spend some time together.

He: I will try.

Me: No trying, its final.

He: Once I'll come, you'll be so irritated within two days that you'll ask me when I will be leaving.

Me: Why so?

He: Oh, my limbs move a lot. :P

Me: We'll have one arm's distance always.

He: When I come there, I promise you there won't be enough distance for air to pass between us.

Me: You and your dreams.

He: Very soon all of them are going to be true.

Me: Okay sir, I will never ask you about when you are going to leave. Alright?

He: Okay, ma'am.

Me: I love you. Please come soon.

He: I love you too.

Me: Perhaps, we'll go for a horror movie.

He: Are you crazy?

Me: Why? It'll be just a movie.

He: Think through, please.

Me: Hehehe, shut up.

And I can't keep my excitement to myself.

Let me dance and celebrate. And sort out my wardrobe.

Rayan Sir and his demands.

Rayan's birthday was around the corner and I wanted to light up the entire city.

I thought of sending him birthday gifts, although neither did he like birthdays nor celebrations. He was against all of this and the strangely he didn't like gifts as well.

I had taken his address slyly form him but when I told him that I'll be sending him something, he outright rejected the idea. He said, "Give me whatever you want to when we meet". But I told him that I had already gotten him the gifts and if he doesn't want them he could very well throw them.

I, of course, knew that Ravz did not like all of this much. But I was dead sure that Ravz would be happy to see what I would send him. And his smile was priceless for me. The happiness that I get out of making him happy, out of listening to his voice filled with love, is beyond explicable.

He told me that Kashmiris don't celebrate birthdays. Close friends and relatives wish them and a few close friends gift them something. That's it. I guess this was a tradition limited to his family or probably it was how things generally went about there.

But I am from Delhi and so I put in my heart and soul into making his birthday special.

Anjali and I went to Pacific mall and bought a watch, a greeting card, a pair of goggles and a perfume. Along with the gifts, I sent a note that read 'Happy Birthday, My Forever.' I bought all those things according to my choice and I was so excited that I ended up spending everything I had. I didn't even have enough money to pay the *rickshaw wallah* to take me from the metro station to my college. I walked to my college from the metro station daily, for at least two weeks.

The gifts I wanted to be delivered on 20th were handed out on 17th. So much for a birthday surprise!

On 17th, he called me up to thank me. I can never forget that conversation.

He: Hey! Got the gifts. Everything is amazing, *Jaan*. Thank you very much. I LOVE YOU A LOT.

Me: If you liked them then I don't want anything else. I LOVE YOU TOO. Wear the watch and send me a picture now

He: Done.

Me: OMG! It's looking lovely.

He: yes, it is… the best gifts ever.

Me: You know they had to be delivered on the 20th, they lied to me.

He: Let it be. How does that make any difference?

Me: It does.

Later, on 21st September, when it was his birthday, I called him up sharp at 12 am. I sang him a birthday song.

I penned down my wishes for him.

"Ravz may god give you all the happiness in the world, everything that you deserve. Please be the same always. I love you the way you are. Today, I want to tell you that I respect you more than I love you, Ravz. You are the only reason for which I live. I am waiting for you every moment to come to Delhi! Ravz, you have made my life beautiful. I just want our careers to settle and then we could be together. I am lucky to have you, Ravz. Thank you".

I wish I would have been there that day with his friends who made his birthday special. From the photos that Rayan sent me, I could see Ravz singing, playing guitar, cutting the cake; I wish I could hug him, be with him… but since he wore the watch I had gifted him, through the watch I was with him despite not being there. I sought peace in the fact that sweet are the fruits of patience and hence I hoped and prayed that henceforth, we'll celebrate all our birthdays together. *In shah Allah*

One thing that I've missed out on is Rayan's passion for music. I always wanted Ravz to try making a career out of singing once he completed his BA LLB. I wanted him to compose a song and record that song. I often said this to Ravz but he always ignored it. Maybe because he knew that his parents would never support him. Although I had tried to convince him that he was doing one thing for his parents, hence the other he should do for himself. And when his parents will realize how good a singer he is, they will never object. I guess he was afraid for no reason; he had never even talked to his parents about this. He had just assumed that they will never consent to it.

A few days later he told me that he had composed a song for me. He hadn't yet completed the song but he sang to me whatever bit was done. I don't even remember the lyrics of the song; maybe because I was lost listening to them. I was so happy; I almost had tears in my eyes. He promised me that he would complete the song and *In Sha Allah* record it as well. I didn't know whether his parents would support him, but he would always find me by his side. Always.

#8 The Pending Doom

Our life was filled with happiness. The only thing we were scared of, were our parents. I had faith that my parents would object at first but then they would agree once they meet Ravz and get to know him. I knew that at the end of the day it was my happiness that mattered to my parents the most. I thought that Allah might show a path and hence I didn't tell him anything. Yes, this was confirmed that if nothing works out, I would convince my parents to let me go to Kashmir.

Ravz efforts were futile. His parents were adamant about the fact that the girl can't be a Delhiite, she had to be a Kashmiri.

One fine day, reality stuck our dreamland and I

woke up to the shock of my life.

*TEXTS*He: What happened?

Me: Nothing, just a bit of a head ache.

He: sleep a little; it'll be fine once you wake up.

Me: I don't feel sleepy right now; I'll tell when you I do.

He: Okay fine.

Me: So, tell me something.

He: I have nothing to tell.

Me: Why? What happened?

He: Nothing.

Me: Okay fine, you know yesterday we enjoyed a lot; all my friends were having fun. We ate a lot and danced a lot.

He: Good for you.

Me: Something isn't okay, what is it?

He: … I was speaking to my family

Me: To Appi?

He: Yes

Me: Did you talk about me? I mean us?

He: Nothing can happen, Alfisha.

Me: What do you mean?

He: I mean that if I talk about you even once more to my parents, I will lose them and their love forever. I LOVE YOU jaan and I don't want to lose you, but I LOVE my

parents too and I can't think of losing them.

Me: I understand your situation Ravz, but if you don't talk or if Appi doesn't talk then how would it work?

He: I don't know. They've clearly said that if I want to live with you then I should forget them.

Me: What?

He: Yes, we have 1 percent chances of being together, if we want to live with this hope then its fine, but if not, we must separate our ways.

Me: What nonsense are you talking? First, all of this isn't just about you. Whenever you feel like you

walk away with the decision that we won't talk now, and now we'd suddenly talk, now I would convince my parents and now they won't listen to me, so let's part our ways. Am I a toy for you? You've turned all of this into some game; whenever you feel like you enter whenever you feel like you leave.

He: What can I do? I have my parents on one side and my love on the other and I can't leave my family.

Me: … and you can leave me?

He: It's not like that; you know very well that I love you.

Me: Then think of some solutions, why are you

taking about breaking up?

He: Can you?

Me: yes.... I am ready to come to Kashmir. I know my parents wouldn't agree easily, but I will convince them. I will learn speaking in Kashmiri and how to cook. Then your mom would accept me or not? I wouldn't give her any reasons to complain.

He: No, the fact that you can speak Kashmiri or not or whether you know how to cook Kashmiri food makes no difference at all. She just wants a Kashmiri girl, that's it.

Me: Ravz, what are you trying to say?

He: I don't want to say anything; I am just getting screwed thinking of what would happen.

Me: Then say at least something. Anything? Don't just keep saying that you don't know what would happen. I am at least thinking of something, giving some suggestions, not sitting mum like you.

He: So, what do I say then? You don't know my parents, I do.

Me: Ravz, leave me.

He: What?

Me: Yes, this is what you are trying to say... you don't have the guts to say it straight off... so I am making it easier for you. Happy?

He: Happy? Are you crazy? Do you even understand what am I going through? Do you have any idea? Do you even know how much I love you? I will die if you are not there. I LOVE YOU. I love you more than I do myself. You aren't my jaan just for the sake of saying it, I really mean it. We decided on forever. You're my forever.

Me: Then, don't leave me.

He: Can I call you?

Me: Yes

PHONE CALL

Ravz- Are you crying?

Me- No. Will you come in January for sure?

Ravz- Yes, jaan, I definitely will.

Me- Promise? I will wait for you.

Ravz- Yes jaan, I will.

Ravz-Say something please.

Ravz- Speak up.

Me- I LOVE YOU, jaan.

Ravz-I LOVE YOU too. Why is all of this happening to us?

Me- Ravz, we should break up. Certain things are just not meant to be, this is one of those.

Ravz- No, please.

Me- Yes.

Ravz- Anything but this.

Me- No.

silence

Me-What happened?

Ravz- I don't want to break up, anything but this.

Me- What do you want? Let fate decide if we should still be together?

Ravz- Yes.

ME- Okay! So what else?

Ravz-Please always stay with me. Please never

give up on me.

Me- I promise, I will never give up on you. I will Pray to Allah, and now even more, and Allah will bring us together, be it today or months later or years later. We've decided on forever and forever you shall be for me. My heart says this Ravz, and if our prayers are true, they are heard, always. In Sha Allah.

Ravz- Yes, we will be together na, jaan.

Me-In Sha Allah, we can just pray this.

Ravz-Hmm.

ME-You won't lose courage, promise me?

Ravz- Yes, I won't. Good night.

That night, I tossed and turned hopelessly.

At 10 in the morning I got Rayan's text.

Ravz Good Morning, Jaan.

Me-Good morning.

Ravz-You slept?

Me-No, I didn't.

Ravz-Neither did I, not at all.

Me-You are fine?

Ravz- I kept thinking about us the whole night.

Me- Please, not again. We did talk about this yesterday. Now when you'll come to Delhi in January, we will talk about this face to face.

Ravz-Tell me one thing. If we aren't together then what? What would you do then?

Me- I will commit suicide. Now say, you got your answer?

Ravz- No. I kept thinking the entire night and I felt we shouldn't risk it on the future. I don't know about you but I will commit suicide now itself.

ME- Stop saying nonsense stuff.

Ravz- I am saying this after a lot of thought.

ME-Ravz, please.

Ravz-Please understand. When my parents get ready for you, I will come back to you. I will never marry anybody else, but if at all the question of my marriage arises, I will clearly say that I will marry just you. And then if they must marry me, they will have to agree to what I say. Then I will come back. But if they don't agree then both of us will die, metaphorically. Let alone mine, but I don't want to risk your life. Please try to understand what I am saying.

Me-Ravz, if you leave me now, will I survive? ...We decided on forever, Ravz.

Ravz- You must; for yourself, for your family.

BLOCKED *BLOCKED*

Since that day my life had taken a dramatic turn. I had nothing in my hands. What could I say to him? Leave your parents and be with me? I couldn't stop him as it meant separating him from his parents. Neither would he have ever done that, nor would I have let him do it.

I had asked him to leave me and end all of this because how long could I see him stressed? He was distancing himself from his parents because of me. Despite being happy, he wasn't happy with me because he wasn't with his family.

I couldn't make his life a living hell just to fulfil my dreams.

He was right in his place about thinking about the future. While a patient girl would have waited for a few months, I still had spent four years. He was thinking of the future and I, of the present.

Yes, after a lot of thought I had supported him in his decision and after a lot of courage I had blocked him as well. But then when I lay down at night I realized that I hadn't eaten food. Then I realized that I was in a habit of asking Ravz if he had eaten or not. Then I looked at my phone.

Now there's nobody who will ask me if I have eaten or not.

Whose messages will I wait for ?

Who will call me Jaan..?

How will I listen to his song..?

Will I never listen to his voice ever again..?

Who will ask for my picture now?

Who will tell me what do I wear at which occasion?

What will I do at night?

Who will I fight with?

Would I never be able to reprimand him for never studying?

Will he never talk love to me again?

All these questions crossed my mind. Then I realized how big a fool I was. How could I let him go?

I could not even live without him.

I picked up the phone, unblocked him and sent him a message. But the messages were not delivered because he had blocked me. I called him, but he didn't pick up my call. I kept calling him and sending him messages. Messages were being delivered, the calls were ringing. But he wasn't replying. And I was finally realizing that the beautiful part of my life was over.

#9 The Struggle

It took me a lot of days to realize that Ravz was no longer in my life. I couldn't eat, I couldn't sleep. I had stopped functioning by then. When I couldn't find peace at night, I kept texting him. I knew he had blocked me and my messages were not being delivered but I was still trying.

One month had passed. At times, I used to wake up at midnight and cry and promise myself that I'll never cry again. Every morning I broke my promise.

Probably the fault wasn't entirely mine because nothing was in my control, not even my heart.

My exams were approaching and I had assignments to submit, something that I never paid heed to because I hardly went to college that month. I used to pray to Allah to give me the strength to go to college and answer my friends, strength to make an excuse without crying. I didn't want my friends to know about my situation, or to fail in a subject and disappoint my family. I had always been a good student and my family had expectations. Going to the college and submitting the assignment was important to me.

It took me a week to prepare myself to attend college for one day. I felt like I was drained-emotionally, mentally and at times physically. Ravz's words, his voice kept echoing in my mind. I kept going back to his texts, his voice notes, his photos; anything that made me feel closer to him. Some people had the good luck to experience closure; I could never find it in me to ask for one.

After days of feeling low, I went to college with a sorry excuse of being ill all this while. Did they buy it? I'm not too sure. After that, I started going to the college regularly. It took me long to realize that I had completely changed. I wasn't going to college just to have fun; I was just going for the sake of it. I used to sit silently during the breaks; alone. I didn't want to speak to anybody, meet anybody, go anywhere; I didn't like anything. People had started thinking I was mean or reserved. And frankly, it didn't bother me.

Coming back home from college, I felt drained. At times, I felt useless. Life had lost its purpose for me. I could not do anything or be myself again. I was in transit, without a clue about the destination I was headed to.

Home felt like a forced prison. I had to smile, speak, behave normally, and stay happy. I was always chirpy and people around me were used to see me like that. My silence stressed them and hence I had to act normal and pretend that I wasn't hurt.

The only thing I thought was-

"Yadein kyun nahi bichhad jati?
Log toh pal me bichhad jate hain....!"

"Why don't memories leave us?
When people take moments to do so....!"

I had lost all my friends who were by my side in college. Staying alone started to add to my misery. One day on my way to the metro, I almost fainted. A school friend, Heena, saved me. Like an angel, she took me to her uncle's hospital. I wasn't conscious enough to realize where I was going. The moment we reached the hospital, I fainted. When I gained consciousness, I had a drip attached to my hand. All this while, I just wanted to hear Rayan's voice. Just, once.

I was in great agony and the reason was not the syringe or my bleeding veins. It was Ravz's behaviour, his indifference; Did our separation not bother him in any way? The doctor kept asking me to keep the phone down, how could I make him understand that none of his medicine could make me feel better but his voice would.

Heena dropped me home. And I went to my room without conversing with anyone. On being asked I told mom that I already had lunch and would like to sleep as I had a headache. I called Ravz and his phone was out of reach; messages were not being delivered. It took me a while to recall that he had blocked me. From now on I couldn't call him either.

Have you ever felt like someone punched you out of the blue and you had no clue how to cope? I was having the same dilemma.

All this while I had a zillion questions crossing my mind. Why did I trust him? Why did I give my life to him? Why? Why at all? How could love end so suddenly? How could a relationship breaking up suck away all emotions? He was my Ravz... How could he let it happen to me?

I wanted to scream and ask Allah, what did I do to deserve this?

When did my tears pave way for my dreams, I have no clue. But at least in my dreams I could have Rayan. I dreamt about him, sitting beside by pillow, stroking my hair and asking me why I was crying. I remember I had a whole conversation with him.

Ravz- Why are you crying?

Me- Because I could not live without you? How could you block me? How could you do this? Why?

Ravz – Jaan, stop crying first, don't you know I can't see you crying?

Me -Ravz if you can't see my tears, why did you leave me?

Ravz -How do I explain my actions? Do you think my love for you is fake?

Me - I know you love me.

Ravz -although we haven't met each other, but don't you feel it? What we have is something special, right?

Me -I have Ravz, every moment.

Ravz - Do you believe in Allah?

Me - The most.

Ravz -Do you want us to live together with Allah's blessings, with our parents' blessings?

Me-Of course, but all this is difficult, what if they don't agree? What will we do?

Ravz -They would agree. If not today, then tomorrow. But with Allah's grace, they will.

Me-Yes Ravz, but...

Ravz- No but, just pray.

Ravz-Whatever I am doing is for the both of us. And you'll have to understand. Alfisha, you'll have to understand.

Me- Hmm....

Ravz- Stay strong, believe in Allah and in our love. All of this is a test and when this is over, we'd have our perfect 'Happily Ever After.' We're in this together. You're my forever. We decided on forever okay? Okay?

Me – Yes, I understand.

Ravz - …And, never doubt my love.

Me- I'm scared.

Ravz- I know. Your pain, your restlessness, your love, your faith; I can feel everything.

Me- Hmm…. I'll pray.

Ravz- So will I.

Me- I really love you

Ravz- I love you too.

When I opened my eyes, there was a strange strength. That dream gave me faith. It answered all my questions. All my confusions were uprooted in that one dream. I had made a firm decision that I will recite the Namaaz five times a day. And I will read the Nafil for Ravz. I had never felt this determined. It was as though Allah had given me a message to be patient through this dream. And I believed this patience would bear the sweetest fruits of my life. Because Allah is indeed always with the patient.

Later, I got out of my room, helped mom cook, ate and slept. I had a firm belief that now when Ravz and I meet, we'll do so with everybody's blessings. And then we'd be together; always.

As weeks passed, I found myself adapting to my situation.

I had to live. One day at a time.

One day, I asked my mom as to what gives people the strength to recite Namaaz every day She said Allah is with those who have nobody. Allah is omnipresent. He always watches us. Everybody believes in Him, few have a belief stronger than others. The ones whose faith is un-wavering are the most sublime human on Earth. So, the people who read Namaaz five times a day, read the Qur'an, are the ones who have faith in Allah, and that He will fulfil all their dreams.

Me- So if we read Namaaz five times a day, all our prayers will be heard.

Mom-Yes. If you do this with complete faith. Then he will.

Me- How much time will it take?

Mom-A day, a week, a month, a year, may be a lifetime.

Me- Really?

Mom- Yes. But Allah always gives what we ask for with a true heart. And the ones Allah loves most are the ones He'd test the most. He just wants to see if obstacles weaken your faith in Him. His tests are tough. The ones who pass them are rewarded with the gift of Allah's acceptance of their prayers. Understood?

Me- Yes, understood.

Mom- Understood what?

Me-That to be Allah's favourite, read the Namaaz, read the Qur'an, believe in Him. Pray and then all your prayers will be heard.

It was now my time to be courageous, to stay strong and to believe. I started praying honestly. Pray that his parents accept us, accept me. All my dreams, small or little were associated with love. I wanted Allah to get us together. After all, they say that Allah loves you like your mother. If you cry and ask him for something with utmost honesty; he'd grant your wishes. Like a mother who grants whatever you want, because she loves you.

Whenever I missed Ravz I used to cry and pray. I had never wanted anything with the intensity that I wanted Ravz. All my tears, all my restlessness and all my pain emanated from just one person.

It had been six months since we had broken up; we had not heard or seen each other.

One day Anjali called me, and asked me to check the audio she has sent me on WhatsApp. I heard it in the night, it was Ravz's voice. It was his self-composed song. The same song he had sung for me, the one whose lyrics were never completed. The moment I heard the song, I started crying, I had no control over my emotions. While I was listening to his song I was thinking it must have been a big day for him. How happy he must have been, I wish I could be with him. I knew not a lot of his family supported him. I wish I could support him, be with him, and make him even more happier. I wish! I wish!

I listened to this song while I slept, while I went to college, while I was home. I was feeling his voice; I could feel his love for me. That song was making me realise that my dream was true, he loved me just as much as I loved him.

#10 New friends and new beginnings

After Inha, it was Saloni and Anjali who ruled my heart and supported me no matter what. With them, I felt like I was at home. At peace. They'd look out for me, no matter what, and for that I was thankful to Allah.

Once I was feeling weak and suffocated so Anjali and I went to the doctor. He said that it was due to lack of sleep and blood would have to be injected. The drip was in my hands and she was the one crying.

Anjali- Why are you doing this?

Me- What?

Anjali- All this (pointing towards my drip).

Forget him, please.

Me- I am fine.

Anjali- I can see how fine you are…

Me- Ugh! See I have been praying day and night. He'll come back to me.

Anjali- Do I tell him of your condition? At least he would talk to you then.

Me - Are you sick? He'll be tensed. I won't even tell you anything again if he gets to know anything.

Anjali- Fucking asshole, you are dying here and still what worries you is that he'll be tensed!

Me- So?

Anjali- Die then.

Me- Don't be angry, please. I know that my pain that is paining you. I swear on you if I could I would have forgotten him. My family is more important for me. I can't help anything; he has gotten in my veins. The moment all of this gets fine, I'll apologise to all of you but for now, please stay with me. I need you. I really do.

Anjali- Fine don't cry now. All will be fine. Stay strong.

Saloni was kept in dark about all of this because she would've freaked out for no reason. I was avoiding meeting her and even speaking to her on the phone because she understood everything just by listening to my voice.

***

People say everything is up to fate, but they forget that prayers can change fortunes. I was not of the sorts who would forget things just by saying he was not in my destiny. I believed that if he is not my destiny, my prayers will force Allah-Ta'la to rewrite my destiny.

With passing time, my restlessness increased, and I was breaking down. I prayed and prayed hard. I prayed that Allah should not let my hopes die. If my hopes break down, I will break down. Masha-Allah I had read fifteen hundred nafils in his name. Praying was peace. But God knows what went wrong this time; because nothing could bring peace, probably because I was missing him or maybe because I was scared. Fear, not because he would forget me but because his parents might get him married. Indeed, it was difficult to get him married but a mom can get her kids do anything. And for Ravz, his family meant everything. If his mother skipped one meal or cried, he would do anything for her. I had told him if his family could convince him to stay away from me, they could pretty well convince him to marry someone else. He did not agree to this then but I knew him more than he knew himself.

When January came, my hopes got a new lease of life. Ravz had said he would come to Delhi between twentieth and twenty-third. I believed that come what may, he will come and if something goes wrong, once I see him, sit with him, hold his hands, all our problems would be sorted.

He had said that he wanted to see me in a frock for the first time; so I got a very pretty, black frock stitched.

All this while, as I was dreaming of my happy days with Rayan, my family was thinking of something else. Traditionally, girls got married off early in my household. Just as the girl reaches second or third year in college, people start sending marriage proposals. My mom felt that this was the right age to get married. Also, the engagement lasted for 2-3 years so that the respective families get to know each other.

I went to a family function once and somebody considered me marriage; and without any delay called my home. They were rich and the guy was educated and his parents liked me. It was a perfect match for me, as per my mom. She was happy. And God knows why, but she thought that probably after a bit of convincing I would agree.

Me- What are you saying Mom?

Mom- Think about it once.

Me -What is it there to think about? Go and say no to them.

Mom - Why would I say no? Would everything always work as per you? You're a kid now, you don't know anything. Whatever parents do, they do it for their kid's happiness.

Me- Exactly my point mom. I am a kid right now; I am in my second year.

Mom- Yes, so I am not saying marry now, just get engaged. You have 2-3 years; you must do your masters. You have all the time. Then marry.

Me -No, Mom. Stop building castles in the air.

Please don't think about it ever again, please.

I could never trust my mother on this, so I dropped a message to the guy. Luckily, he was in love with someone else. And so, we ended everything.

With all the drama that was happening in my life, I kept looking forward to that one day when I would finally meet my Rayan.

I knew Ravz's train would stop at Delhi. He had told me this, a hundred times. So, I wore the black frock and went to the old Delhi railway station. I reached around 10 and started calling him, thinking that he would have unblocked me. But I was still blocked. At first, I thought he might have forgotten; like he forgot my birthday once.

It was now six in the evening, and there was no trace of Ravz. He should have reached by the afternoon. I though the train could be late. By seven, I started showed his photograph to the workers there, asking them if they had seen him that day. I had to leave. I repeated the same drill the next day. And the next.

Twenty-Third January was my last hope. I

reached the station at seven in the morning. Even the people around had recognized me by now. They looked at me with pitying eyes and asked who I was waiting for. I didn't have an answer to their question then, and neither do I now. If we weren't in a relationship, then who was I waiting for? I just looked at them with teary eyes and asked them to just pray that whomever I am waiting for, just comes.

All the courage that I gathered over the past one year shattered with the clock striking seven. I started crying and screaming. I was just asking Allah, why did he not come? He had promised me he would.

What will I do now? What will I say to mom and dad? What do I say to console myself and what lies do I tell my heart? I had lost on myself, on my heart. What do I do? Why was nobody helping me? People say that poverty is the worst. I say helplessness is. When somebody wants to do something but they can't. When your heart defeats you, when your heart won't let you do anything. That moment I was helpless. People were staring at me and I was crying and talking to myself like a mad person. I was shouting at every person who made eye contact with me.

I had lost all hope that day. Probably because I couldn't see him or listen to him ever gain. Everything was so dramatic. I had fever and I couldn't sleep the entire night. I was hoping that he would appear through thin air and take me away.

Since that day, I wasn't the same Alfisha.

"Iska gham nahi tha ki 'usne' barbaad kiya,
Gham iska tha ki, bahut der ke baad kiya."

I couldn't understand what do I do? How do I console myself? How do I control my tears?

What was my fault? That I loved him or that I loved a Kashmiri guy?

I should hate that person, right? I should be angry with him. But my heart was not ready to accept that.

"Bada ajeeb hota hai yeh mohabbat ka khel,
koi ek thak jaye to dono haar jate hai."

#11 Living with broken dreams

Whoever said "Never judge a book by its cover" had to be the wisest man, who had experienced life like no other. Looking back, if I had known things would have turned out like this, I would have never fallen for that sly smile and droopy eyes. I would have never fallen for Rayan.

When a girl falls in love with a person, she forgets everything else in the world. The only thing that matters is that one special person to whom she gives her heart and soul. But boys… they don't have it in them to love like that! It is a notion that in the 21st century, girls treat relationships as though it was a game of some kind, they change boyfriends as though they were changing clothes… moving on is nothing for them. And yes, there probably are some girls of this kind. But not every girl is like this right. Why don't we ever talk about those girls who live their entire lives with the name of that one person engraved in their hearts? A boy, who was once serious about a girl, still finds it in him to move on when they've broken off but it's not the same in a girl's case. The word "moving on" doesn't find a place in her dictionary.

Rayan may have given up, but I never did. Somewhere deep down I always knew that one day Allah will make everything alright. I never let my prayers and faith in him falter, lest he did not fulfill my wish!

Every night I called him, texted him in the hope that maybe, he'd decide to unblock me and I'd finally get a chance to talk to him, get a chance to find out what he wanted, know what was going on in his heart, get some clarity on what he was thinking, why he didn't come to Delhi, why he was so helpless, what were his constraints. Why in the world was he doing this?!

I needed the answers to all these questions. Almost as if my life depended on the answers to these questions.

One fine day, he did unblock me.

I was on WhatsApp in the night and I realized Ravz had unblocked me. I cannot express in words what I felt when I saw his DP. The satisfaction that washed over me was beyond expression. His DP was the picture of his hand with the letters RA inked in bold on it.

I remember he always had the habit of doodling on the back pages of his register. He would then send me the pictures of what he'd made or written and I would never miss an opportunity to make a joke on it! Little did I know that this very habit of his would one day bring so much content in my life!

He probably unblocked me for this very reason, so I could see his DP. And probably in his own way, even tell me that he still loves me.

I texted him.

Me: Ravz… I LOVE YOU A LOT. And don't worry! If you feel your aren't ready or that this isn't the right time for us to be together, it's okay… don't stress yourself over it! I will still be waiting here for you.

(Seen)

Me: You just take care of yourself. And don't worry about me. I'm doing just fine.

(Seen)

He read the two messages of mine and left it at that. Though I knew I wouldn't be getting any reply to the messages, deep down I thought he'd be happy. After all, "RA" was short for Rayan and Alfisha. Right?

I was so happy that in that moment I truly believed that everything had become perfect once again and that he had finally come back to me and this time it was forever and ever. I immediately read two 'nafil shukrane' prayers and thanked Allah Ta'la for guiding me during my difficult times.

I know this seems like a very small or rather insignificant incident but for me it was the greatest thing that had happened in ages. It was the victory of my faith, my hope, my conviction and nothing could be better than that. This was like an indication from Allah that I was on the right track and more importantly that 'he' was with me.

I started believing that Allah was now with me, Ravz's love was with me and soon enough our family, our elders, too would give us their blessings.

The whole night I kept looking at his DP and he probably was looking at mine. I was so lost in his thoughts that I can't even remember when I fell asleep.

When I woke in the morning I found myself blocked again. But honestly speaking, I kind of expected it. I know him way too well.

"Usko meri bahaut yaad aarahi hogi… bechaini ho rahi hogi use isliye usne wo DP lagayi aur mujhe unblock bhi kiya usne, taaki mai use dekh pau aur reply karu. Usse mera yeh reply dekhkar khushi toh bahaut hui hogi lekin woh iss baat ko maanega nahi. Woh soch raha hoga ki shitt…! Mai kamzor kaise padh gaya? Mai itna kamzor kaise padh sakta hu ki aur use ek nayi umeed de di!

Ab aage agar fir bhi kuch nahi ho paya toh? Woh marr jayegi…!

Block fir dubara iss guilt me kiya usne ki usne mujhe unblock kyu kiya. Aur iss darr se bhi ki kahi aage maine dubara message kar diya aur use control nahi ho paya toh fir kya hoga? Mai toh ek ladka hu… sambhal lunga lekin woh kaise sambhalegi?"

It was this fear festering inside of him that acted

like a wall between us. Rayan used to get scared of situations very fast. He would let all the negativity and fear take over him every time he thought of our future. I wish he understood that if we were together, if we stood by each other always, then one day or another his parents would understand and accept us.

I was ready to leave everything, my parents, my friends, my home, town, my dreams, everything, for him. I had this much confidence in myself and in our love that I'd win over the hearts of his family one day. If Ravz was with me, I could handle any problem as difficult as it would be.

If I could possess such courage and faith, why couldn't he? Why was he so afraid?

I wish Allah would bless him with some courage too. At least with as much as is necessary so that he could take one step for me... "Hamaare liye."

Months later, as I watched the news, I saw that there was a rise of water level in Kashmir. I pleaded with Allah to show mercy and make everything alright. To calm myself, I sent Ravz a very normal message and two minutes later I received a delivery report.

This in fact was an amazing thing. With this simple report, I got to know two things; first, he unblocked my number and second, he was in Pune, because messages don't get delivered in Kashmir.

I couldn't control myself when I heard that Kashmir was in the Danger Zone and I immediately dialled Ravz. I really thought he'd take my call this time. If for no other reason than for the fact that he'd know way too well how tensed I'd be. The last time we were in the same situation, it wasn't him but rather I who began crying for his family.

Thank god, he received my call. He was probably on the bike when he took my call because I could hear a lot of traffic in the background. Both of us kept saying hello but the sound of all the traffic in the background was so loud that we couldn't hear each other.

Then all of a sudden, his voice became clear and he asked if it was 'Isha' on the line?

Isha? Who was this Isha? Had he already forgotten my voice? So fast?

He didn't even have my number saved?

How could he forget me?

So many questions came to my mind after hearing just one name. I gathered all the courage I had in me, kept my voice in control and replied "Nahi, main Isha nahi Alfisha bol rahi hu."

He went silent the minute he heard my name. For two long minutes, both of us were quiet and then I asked him if all was fine at home. I asked him if his family was safe.

I just managed to say this much and he cut my call. I tried calling back many times but he didn't answer my calls.

Then I messaged him saying that if he didn't want to talk then so be it but at least let me know if his family was fine and safe. I wouldn't trouble him anymore after that.

But he never replied.

Why was he acting like this? What did he want to achieve by doing these things?

I failed to understand.

After a long time, when I couldn't acquire any news, I started reciting the tahajjud. There is a saying that anything prayed for during the tahajjud namaaz is always granted. At that time my prayers were only for Ravz's family. I prayed with my whole heart for their safety, I prayed to Allah Ta'la to protect them from all their problems.

Kashmir no longer faced any fears now as the water levels had dropped down. But what about the fears in my heart? When would my fears rest and my problems come to an end?

What should I derive from those two minutes of silence?

Maybe there was some meaning attached to that silence that I could not understand yet. There were just two lines I could think of at that time;

"Tu khamosh kyu hai yeh to maloom nahi magar,
dil doob sa jata hai jab tu khamosh hota hai."

I always believed that Ravz would never give the place I had in his life to anyone else. It was because of this trust and faith I had in him that I always prayed to Allah, asking him to help me get accepted by Ravz parents. I never asked Allah to always maintain the love Rayan had for me. Never in my wildest dream did I think that Rayan did not think on the same lines as I did… or that he wanted to move on… or that someone else could take my spot in his life, who maybe makes him happier than I did. I never thought of these things before. Though now I feel I should have considered these possibilities before.

Despite my disapproval, Saloni and Anjali used to keep an eye on Rayan. Saloni always felt he would never wait for me, rather he'd move on at the first opportunity he'd get. They tried their level best to explain this to me, but I never listened to them. In fact, one day she even told me that she'd bring me proof that to Rayan; I was someone he dated in the past and nothing more. She often told me I destroying my own life with my very hand, digging my own grave, and the day I realized that, It would have been too late.

It was my unfortunate luck that Saloni was right, and this time she came home with proof. She opened Rayan's timeline on Facebook and made me read the comments on every picture of his.

There was this girl "Alisha" from Kashmir who had commented on every single picture of his with I LOVE YOU JAAN, MERA ZUWA, MY BABY, and MUAAAAHHHH…it wasn't the comments that shocked me, but Rayan's replies. In a very loving tone, he replied to each comment with an I LOVE YOU TOO JAANU, MUAAAHHHH…. MISS YOU and what not!

It felt as though someone had pulled the rug from under my feet. I immediately opened Alisha's timeline but everything was blocked except for her status which read "in a relationship with Rayan." Her DP too was one of Rayan's childhood pictures, which at one point of time was one of my favourite pictures of his. On that picture too, Rayan had commented asking her why she wasn't replying on WhatsApp and to do so soon.

Was this all a bad dream or was this really happening to me?

I kept praying that this was a bad dream and very soon I would wake up from it. But this wasn't a dream… it was the truth… a very bitter truth. I was shattered, and broken beyond repair. I didn't know what to do, what to say… I was so quiet, as if my lips had been sealed. I wanted to cry, but I just couldn't. As if my tears too were in a state of shock.

After pacifying me, Saloni left. But where do I go from here? I kept asking myself this question again and again… where do I go now?

For whom was I praying? For this guy who didn't even remember me? For this person, I was head over heels in love! Who probably forgot me long back and has already moved on?

"JAAN", that word. I always thought that only I had the right to use it. Did he?

My trust, faith, hope… all existed only till the time I believed that he loved me. What do I ask Allah for now?

"Alisha and Rayan" maybe that's what Allah Ta'la wants. Maybe that's his will. Maybe this is what Rayan deserves. Maybe it's better for him this way. Actually, this is better for him. That girl is from Kashmir… loves Rayan and most importantly he is very happy with her.

What else does anyone want?

His parents are happy and so is he. And if I do love him, I should be happy for him. I always asked Allah to keep him happy. I never kept any condition when I asked Allah for his happiness. Now when Allah accepted my prayers, who am I to find faults in them?

He managed to move on, that was his good luck. I couldn't and that was my weakness.

What took over me? How could I cry for such a person? Who didn't even think about me once…

who didn't even think it necessary to find out if I was alive or dead! Everything was right in front of me, everything was crystal clear, but still my heart wasn't ready to believe that he could cheat on me.

"Ye mujhe chain kyu nahi parta,
Ek hi shaks tha jahaan me kya?"

All the proof of his betrayal was right in front of my eyes… and I repeatedly read it to get myself to hate him for what he had done to me!

He perhaps will never even realize to what extent he has hurt me. Every dream of mine, small or big revolved around him, even though we were far apart I did everything a girl madly and crazily in love would do. His laughter, that smile on his face always held highest priority in my life. I loved him more than my own life; my love for him was beyond any promises and beyond any oaths.

But what did I do wrong? Where did I fall short?

How could he have forgotten me?

How?

I cried so much that my eyes began to swell up. Switching places from my bathroom to my room and then again from my room to bathroom… that's how I spent my whole night. I began feeling nauseous and soon enough began vomiting. Tears wouldn't stop rolling down my cheeks. I felt like I had lost everything I had. Everywhere I looked now, only darkness greeted me.

They say when Allah Ta'la closes one door; he opens ten new and better doors in exchange. I was trying to look for those doors but found nothing but darkness everywhere.

That was by far the worst night I had till date. When mummy saw me in the morning she said, "Beta kitna soti hai tu. So-soker tune apni aakhein suja li hai."

I didn't have any answer to give mummy that day. From that day to today I have remained quiet. I feel ashamed to even tell anyone what happened. I wondered what people would say, maybe something like what a crazy girl is she, got fooled so easily. I thought people would laugh at me and my love for him

I knew I was not in control of myself and my situation and I realized that I wouldn't be able to hide my state from my family for long and this would create tension in the house. So, I cooked up an excuse and went to stay over at Anjali's place for the next two-three days. Anjali told my family that I was going with her family on a vacation. Anjali and I are childhood friends, which is why our parents trust each other.

I wanted some peace so that I could think things through. Where I could find the right path for myself. For two whole days, I was quiet and in a deep thought. I reminisced about everything, my conversation with Ravz, his songs, his promises and that awful dream!

I kept recollecting, kept thinking and kept praying to Allah Ta'la to help me and show me the right way! I pleaded with him to enlighten me on what is right and wrong. And if I were on the wrong path, then to guide me to the right one.

After two days, Saloni too came over to Anjali's place. Both wanted to know what I had finally decided.

Saloni: Can we talk?

Anjali: Yeah… say something.

Me: Yes, I'm fine.

Anjali: What have you decided?

Me: I did deliberate a lot. Some things I thought about from my heart and some from my head

Saloni: Hmm… so what did you ultimately decide?

Me: That he is lying. It's a farce and nothing more.

Anjali: WTF… is this? What are you talking about?

Saloni: Have you lost it? Why would he lie?

Me: Because he wants me to see all this and start hating him. He doesn't want me to love him; rather he wants me to hate him.

Saloni: You've gone mad and that's just it. I cannot make sense of anything you're saying

Me: See… he thinks by doing all this I'll get hurt and one day I'll start hating him for it.

Then as time passes by I'll move on in life.

Anjali: So, that girl "Alisha" is a lie? Is she imaginary?

Me: Maybe or maybe not.

Saloni: Talk some sense, please.

Me: Anjali do you remember Vartika? When his

parents rejected our relation, he was very disturbed and he wanted to forget me, ignore me, which is why he started talking to Vartika, so he could divert his mind. But nothing of the sort happened and he came back to me. Which means this time too he has done this to divert his mind and to make me forget him. It could also be that the girl doesn't even exist in the first place.... Rayan is doing all this only to fool me.

Saloni: Enough! Are you done?

Anjali: Yeah... absolutely madam. Or then it could also be that she is really his girlfriend and the two of them are very happy together. And you here are living in a bubble, dying for him.

Me: No. Trust me, it's not like that!

He is an idiot. He honestly thinks I'll hate him... stupid, idiot, fool. Even if I want to, I can't get myself to hate him. This is nothing; even if he hurts me with something a thousand times worse, I won't be able to get myself to hate him.

Saloni: This is all foolishness. Because you're so madly in love with him, you're cooking up stories to suit yourself.

Me: No, Saloni. I was in a relationship with him for four years.... I know him better than he knows himself. I understand what he does and why he does it. Trust me guys... I can be wrong about anyone, but not about him.

Anjali: Ufff! Why can't you just forget him?

Me: Haha. That's a funny suggestion.

"Main? aur usko bhula du?
Kaisi baate karti hai yaar,
surat toh fir surat hai,
wo naam bhi pyara lagta hai.

Saloni: I don't get this philosophy of yours.

Anjali: Okay... even if we take your word for it that he loves you only, even you agree surely that without his parents' permission, he'll never come back to you?

Me: Hmmm.... He won't.

Saloni: Then?

Me: Then nothing. I'll continue praying for my 'someday.' Because we have decided on our forever.

Anjali: How can you not understand the reality? What are you thinking? How will we be able to understand you or help you if you don't tell us?

Me: I can't understand what his parents want. I've told them I'll come to Kashmir, I'll learn Kashmiri, their rituals, learn how to make their food; everything. I assured them I won't make any mistakes or give anyone a chance to criticize me. But at least give me that one chance…everyone gets at least one chance in life, then why not me?

What sin have I done? What am I guilty of? Say? Why are they doing this to me? Can someone at least tell me my mistake… someone tell me my fault please.

Why am I getting punished in such a way? To such an extent, that I'm finding it so difficult to hold myself together now. Why aren't they understanding Anjali? I'll put my heart and soul to please them, to win their hearts. But at least see me once… talk to me once…without meeting me, or even knowing me, how can they wreck my life?

I know he will be happy with me forever. And do you know why I'm so sure of it? Because I know we both love each other beyond words. I can never hurt him or for that matter any person associated with him. Even if I want to, I won't be able to. I know I am at this state today only because his parents were not ready to accept me. Still I can't think badly about them. My heart won't give me permission to do so. None of this is in my control. And I know you guys think I'm mad. You must be thinking I'm saying all this because I'm emotional. But trust me I'm saying the truth and nothing else.

Saloni: I hope your prayers get answered. Tell me something honestly though… do you really think that Rayan was not to blame for whatever happened?

Me: Are you mad? Of course, he is to blame. In fact, he is the biggest culprit in this whole affair.

Anjali: But, isn't he just helpless in front of his parents?

Me: Oh, really Anjali? Do you remember when I accepted his proposal, I had only two conditions. The first being that I wasn't one among those girls who would say yes just to kill time. Moreover, I warned him that he was from Kashmir and I was from Delhi; our backgrounds are very different.

Saloni: What did he say then?

Me: He said he wasn't a child and he knew what he was doing.

Anjali: And what was the second condition?

Me: the second thing I told him was that here it wasn't only about him or me, but also about his parents. They too probably had some dreams regarding him, some hopes that he'll be with a Kashmiri Girl. Maybe they even have someone in mind. Who knows? Will they accept a girl from Delhi?

Anjali: And what did he reply?

Me: He said that, *"Maine pehle hi ghar mein bola hua tha ki main apni pasand Ki ladki se shaadi karunga. Aur unhe iss baat se koi problem nahi hai. Khushi se accept karenge sab tumhe."*

Saloni: Are you serious? He said this?

Me: Exactly! Now tell me whom should I blame? He came into my life on his terms and left because of the wishes of his parents. My feeling didn't matter to him, at all?

Saloni: Honestly speaking, I can't understand him or his parents.

Me: Haha… frankly, neither can I. All I can say is the image people have of Delhi girls isn't very good. Small town people think that girls from Delhi are very cunning, who make guys fall in love with them, and cast spells over their sons.

Anjali: …But he didn't even glance at you once before just walking out of your life. He's going behind your back and dating girls. Knowing this, how can you still love him so much?

Me: I ask myself the same questions sometimes. But you know what… you fall in love without thinking or contemplating. Every person has some positives and some negatives in them. And when you fall in love with someone you learn to handle their negative points as well. It's true he didn't tell me his parents wouldn't accept me. But it was because till the very end, he hoped that his parents would agree. He didn't want to leave me. There are many times in life when we know the truth, yet we lie to ourselves and those close to us too…because we don't want to upset them. Rather we want to keep them happy. And I can say this so confidently because I have been in such situations too. And the part where, *"usne mujhe mudkar bhi nahi dekha"* happens, to that all I'll say is that people have different ways of loving and showing their love to others. Rayan doesn't know how to express his love in words.

Anjali: Are you sure that he'll come back?

Me: Of course, I am! I have full confidence in myself and on my love. He may take some time but he'll come. In Sha Allah!

Saloni: I hope that day comes fast, and then we'll all celebrate together.

Me: Ameen.

#12 To being Alfisha again

For most people, one year just flies by. But my time is frozen. I'm still stuck in the past with memories of Rayan to cushion me.

Another year passed by waiting for Rayan. I woke up every morning, with the hope that he may just call me today…or maybe text me and my life will again become alright. Every time I got a call from an unknown number, I hoped it was Rayan. But my hopes were proved wrong again and again, when I didn't get even a single reply to the hundred messages that I sent him every day.

Negative thoughts haunted me. I would wake up at midnight sometimes and begin crying. His memories made me weak. For how long was I supposed to put up with all this? For how long can you expect a person to be patient? It had been two years and I was losing my patience now. All my friends were enjoying with their boyfriends… they'd go on dates, celebrate birthdays together, would go shopping together and all I did was stand there with a fake smile on my face, hoping that one day I too would find my happiness.

My world was a different place. I didn't go out much with my friends or family. Staying alone, I wrote my diary and read my novels. That's how I kept myself busy. My friends used to operate my Facebook account. They would forcefully take my pictures and upload it on my Facebook page. They said by doing so everyone would believe that I was fine and doing well in life. Though I didn't care about what others thought, I could never say no to them. Because if I opposed them, they would bombard me with a million questions whose answers I did not have the courage to give. Not only Anjali and Saloni; whoever asked me to do anything, I quietly obeyed. This had become my life.

I had changed completely in these past two years. My family at one time used to call me the world's biggest drama queen; strangely enough, my life itself today had become one big drama.

The only thing that didn't change in the past two years was my prayers. Even today I cry in front of Allah and spreading my arms, I ask him to accept my prayers and give me one chance to prove myself, to live my life, to fulfil my dreams.

Every time I saw others happy, I would wonder why I'm in such a situation. I would think either Allah Ta'la was testing me or I had committed such a crime that he couldn't forgive me! Then I'd say my forgiveness prayers and ask Allah not to give me such a big punishment for the mistakes I made unknowingly.

Please forgive me Allah Ta'la.

Forgive me please… please!

There also came a time when I believed that happiness was not something that was written in my life. I always prayed for Rayan. I wished with all my heart that Allah Ta'la would bring my life back to me, that Allah would show some mercy, some pity on me and answer my prayers. But I was so broken at that time that I didn't ask Allah for Rayan, rather I asked him to give me patience.

I prayed that if this was my destiny then so be it, but at least then give me the strength to face this reality. Give me the strength to forget him, to make my life better and to move on. I prayed for the same thing every night but my wish was never granted.

I wanted to forget him; I didn't even want him to be present in my thoughts or dreams… which is why I threw away all those things which reminded me of him. I deleted all his photos, his chats, the screenshots and all his songs. I tried my level best, did everything I could to forget him. But I think my destiny didn't want that either. Every second thing reminded me of him, of us, of "what could have been."

I remember I would sit by myself at times and out of nowhere I would hear Rayan's voice. I would hear the songs he used to sing for me. I would close my ears as tightly as I could. But his voice would still reverberate in my ears.

I would start sobbing and beg Rayan to leave me alone.

I was like a living zombie.

There are some incidents that leave you altered in a manifold way. I could breathe, but I didn't feel alive. I wanted to forget him but couldn't. I was a victim to my heart!

I would get very angry with myself at times. Why did I cry so much for him? From where did I find so many tears? Was this going to be my destiny forever?

Another year filled with prayers, tears and question passed.

Maybe Allah had new plans for me this year, as I met Zubair.

He considered himself a stud and to an extent he was one too. Girls were crazy for him and he was very proud of that. He was smart, good looking and rich…and as per him, girls looked for these three qualities in guys. And he had all three.

Our first meeting was quite unusual. I was in a rickshaw, around the time of chhoti Holi, and I found myself to be the target of at least three or four balloons. I kept asking the rickshawala to go as fast as he could and covered myself with my dupatta, when I started feeling cold. Just then a car stopped right in front of me. There were three people in the car and the person sitting at the back had a bucket filled with water balloons that he was throwing on passers-by.

I understood that I was their next target the minute they stopped the car in front of my rickshaw.

The boy took one balloon in his hand and looked in my direction. The minute we had eye contact I laughed and said, "Please no… please!" He too started laughing and took out the smallest balloon from the bucket. I then showed him my dupatta which was fully drenched. He understood and finally didn't throw the balloon at me.

When the light turned green, we parted ways.

This was our first meeting, where without knowing each other, without speaking, we understood each other. I never thought we would meet again until…

It was Anjali's parents' 25th anniversary and she threw a grand party to celebrate it. Anyone and everyone was invited. The party's dress code was Indian, so the two of us came dressed in sarees. We were wondering how we'd manage the guests, when we couldn't even handle our own sarees.

I was tending to the guest when I happened to notice that boy whom I met on chhoti Holi. I thought I should at least thank him for what he did on that day. But when I reached him, I happened to overhear his conversation.

He was talking to his friends about girls, as if they weren't humans but some things to bring joy to one's heart. He was telling his friends how he would take a new girl out every day. I honestly wanted to give him one tight slap and throw him out of the party. But then again, neither was this my home and nor my party…it was Anjali's. On top of that, I didn't even know who he was.

I was about leave when Anjali came and introduced the two of us.

Anjali: He is Zubair, an old neighbour and a great friend too.

Zubair: Hi…Your good name?

Me: I don't want to be a part of this.

Anjali: Shut up! Zubair, she is Alfisha, my best friend.

Zubair: I think I've seen you somewhere before.

Me: I don't think so.

Anjali: You guys continue talking…I'll be back in a minute.

Me: Wait…I'm coming too.

Zubair: On chhoti Holi? Right? Yes, you are the same person.

Me: …Okay, can I leave now?

Zubair: Are you feeling hot or are you by nature this hot headed?

Me: Save it for your text 'time pass.'

Zubair: So, that's it. It's wrong to eavesdrop ma'am.

Me: Do you really think that falling in love is a joke for every girl? That it's a time pass for them?

Zubair: All my girlfriends are like that.

Me: Not everyone's like that.

Zubair: I may not know you but I know them and their nature.

Me: well…I think I'm wasting my time. Enjoy the party. Bye.

Zubair: you probably lost all your school debates. Running away from conversations is the easiest thing to do.

Me: Excuse me?

Zubair: Yes please…

Me: What if I prove you are wrong, then?

Zubair: I'll do whatever you ask me to do.

Me: Ok...I want the number of all your girlfriends.

Zubair: ...Alright.

Me: Anjali, type one message "Hey Beautiful. I am Rahul. Zubair's friend. Just want to tell you that Zubair is cheating on you. *Mazze maar raha hai woh bass. Sirf time pass kar raha hai. Ek number ka kutta, kamiya, ullu ka patha hai woh. Tumhare saath saath aur bhi bahaut ladkiyon ko date kar raha hai woh.* I can send you the pictures also if needed. So don't even try to think about your future with him."

Have you typed it?

Anjali: ...Yes.

Me: Good. Now send this message to these girls. If they aren't serious we'll get to know by their reaction, I hope. Right?

Zubair: Ahaan.

Anjali: Sent.

Me: Any replies, Anjali?

Anjali: Yes, three of them have replied!

• Pooja- See… I'm not at all thinking about our future. We are both enjoying our present and that's what matters.

• Radhika- Hahaha… why are you over reacting? It's totally fine with me. We give each other space, so chill.

• Zoya- I already know all this. Even I have best friends… I mean 'bed friends with benefits.' We both are living our lives the way we want.

Zubair: (starts laughing)

Me: 'Friends with benefits'! What the hell is this? I don't believe this!

Me: Stop laughing, please.

Anjali: …Umm there is another message from Ariba.

Ariba- "Excuse me. It's impossible. Rubbish you are talking. Zubair aisa bilkul nahi hai aur hum dono ek dusre se bahaut pyaar karte hai. Bade wade kiye hai usne mujhse aur, saath sapne dekhe hai humne, apne future ki. Toh please aise ghatiya mazak aap dubara kabhi mat kariyega. Na mujhe aapki koi jhoote photos dekhne hai aur na aapki jhooti baate sunni hai. I trust him completely."

Me: FINALLY.

Anjali: Zubair…?

Me: Mr. Zubair Ahmed, whether it's the 19th century or the 21st, love will always remain the same. It doesn't change with time. Even if we accept what you say, three of the four girls are perhaps like you. But did you ever think even once about that one girl who is different? Not every person is the same. I hope you got my point.

Zubair: Hmmm.

Anjali: Now you'll have to do whatever Alfisha asks you to. Come on Alfisha…what do you want him to do?

Me: He should go and apologize to that girl and till the time she doesn't forgive him, Allah wouldn't either. You have broken her heart.

Zubair: Hmmm.

Anjali: come now… let's eat something.

As we went to the food stalls, I felt myself getting a second lease at life. I didn't let go. I didn't want to. Like I never wanted to, two years ago.

The anniversary was closely followed by my birthday.

And I invited all my friends, whom I had barely spoken to in the past two years, to a restaurant near my college, for a party. Everyone came and we were waiting for Anjali.

Anjali: Sorry I know I'm late. It's because of Zubair though.

Me: Zubair?

Zubair: Hey …Happy Birthday!

Me: Why are you here?

Zubair: To wish you.

Me: Thank you very much. Now?

Zubair: Yaar, it is your birthday party… if your friends don't come, then who will?

Me: Friends?

Zubair: Do you mean to say I should leave?

Me: Ummm…the other day, you didn't throw that water balloon on me and I didn't thank you for it. This is my token gesture.

Zubair: Thank you very much.

Anjali's bringing Zubair to the party and her hushed manner of talking to Saloni was a clear indication to me that something was cooking. They wanted me and Zubair to be together. Anjali had already told him about my past which is why he was probably being this sweet to me. The icing on the cake was that they finally found a Muslim boy for me and their excited expressions revealed all the planning that had gone behind this development.

My birthday turned out to be better than I thought and the star of the evening was none other than Zubair. The whole day he made people laugh. I kept insulting him on every small thing but he never reacted. God knows why?

After my birthday, every time I met Anjali and Saloni, Zubair was always present. And as usual, he was always the uninvited guest. Since Anjali and Saloni were accompanied by their boyfriends, Zubair and I were forced to give each other company. We never really spoke…we just fought!

Looking at him made me feel like I was looking at an old mirror, that showed the young and naïve

Alfisha: a chatter box, one who laughed and made others laugh and considered herself perfect.

There are very few people who I judged incorrectly and Zubair was one of them. I got to see a new side of him; at times very bold side, at times scary, and sometimes even cowardly.

Though we never spoke much, we got to understand each other better. He took care of all my needs. He knew my likes and dislikes, my favourite places, favourite actors and everything else related to me. I could sense his affinity towards me.

But Anjali's told him everything about me…then why is he acting so? I was confused and irritated. I didn't know how to tell Zubair that what he wanted, I could never give. What should I have said?

One day, he got me a gift saying that it was a token of our new friendship. Without even thinking twice I said something that I regret to this day. *"Mr. Zubair Ahmed aap apne aap ko samajhte kya hai? Agar aapke paas daulat hai toh kya iska matlab yeh hai ki aap jab chahe doosro ke jazbaat ka khayal kiye bagair unke izzat nafs mazrooh karte rahein? Kabhi Anjali ko gift, toh kabhi Simran, toh kabhi Saloni, aur ab mai? Mujhe aise logo se nafrat hai jo sirf apna rupiya paisa dikhane aur doosro ko unki aukaat jatane kenliye unhe tohfe dete hai; taaki woh aapse mutassir hojayein, aapke aage peeche firein aur aap un per kabhi kabhi taras khaker apni inayaat unpar tohfo ki surat mai nazil karde."*

He left without saying anything.

Anjali and Saloni looked at me with wide eyes.

By the time I realized what had I done, it was too late.

I was hurt. I was in pain. And all my frustrations and anger got directed to Zubair. I know he didn't deserve it. But I'm human. A human who made a terrible mistake.

…A human who was determined to get her new friend back.

And so, I called up Zubair.

Me: Hey! Can we talk?

Zubair: No, we can't.

Me: Zubair you know everything about my past. Then why did you have to do all this?

Zubair: Hmmm….

Me: What hmmm? Say something please? See I'm sorry. I shouldn't have said all those things. I said too much in my rage. Sorry.

Zubair: I'll forgive you on one condition. You'll have to truthfully answer a question of mine. Just say what's in your heart.

Me: Okay done.

Zubair: Hmmm… Alfisha, it's been two years now. Why can't you forget him?

Me: Can we talk about something else, please?

Zubair: No, we can't. You have to answer me!

Me: ….

Zubair: Speak up.

Me: …

Zubair: Just forget him and move on.

Me : *"Woh bewafaa hi sahi lekin abhi Toh umar padhi hai use bhulane ke liye."*

Zubair: When you know that he let you down, then why are you still waiting for him? Why?

Me: ….. *"Woh bewafaa hargis na tha, yun hi badnam ho gaya.*
Hazaro chahne wale thhe, kis kis se wafa karta?"

Zubair: Be practical please. What do you keep thinking about, day and night? Hmm?

Me: *"Woh mera sab kuch hai, bas mera mukaddar nahi, kash woh mera kuch bhi na hota sirf mukaddar hota."*

Zubair: This won't work. You can't go on like this. Anjali has told me all that you've gone through. How much you've suffered. How are you living? Don't you have heart?

Me: *"Kaise batau naksha apni tanhaayi ka,*
ek kayamat hai jo har roz guzar jaati hai."

Zubair: I must say you're a very strong girl, but I can't understand what you want now.

Me : HIM.

Zubair: Allah! He'll never come back. You're spoiling your own life. Can't you see that! You're making a terrible mistake.

Me: Mistake? Loving someone deeply and waiting for that person is not a mistake, according to me.

"Khataa toh jab ho ke haal-e-dill kissi se kahein,
kissi ko chahate rehna, koi khata toh nahi."

Zubair: I'm speechless really. So, what have you decided for the future?

Me: M.A

Zubair: By the way, you are a mind-blowing shayar, I must say.

Me: Thank you.

Zubair : Waise thoda bahut main bhi kar leta hun.

Me: Irshaad Irshaad!

Zubair: *"Uski bewafai par fida hote hai is kadar jaan tere,*
khuda jaane agar usne wafa ki hote toh tera kya hota."

Me: What I'm going through is something you'd never understand.

Zubair: I understand everything.

Me: Everything?

Zubair: *"Tere mohabbat ki, tere saleeke ki daad deta hu,*
uska zikr roz karte hai, uska naam liye bagair."

Me: Allah ! It's my story. Why you are getting so emotional?

Zubair: I've met many kinds of people in my life, seen many types of girls. But I've never met someone like you. You know when I lost that bet the other day, I went to Ariba. When I told her the truth, she cried a lot. That was the first time I saw a girl cry for me and I'll never be able to forgive myself for that. Why don't you do something? Scare Rayan so bad, that he'll have no option but to come back to you?

Me: *"Khairaat mai mili khushi mujhe acchi nahi lagti, mai apne dukhon main rehti hu nawaabon ki tarah."*

Zubair:

"Humein tere wafa se, mohabbat se,
mohabbat hai, kash yeh hamare liye bhi hota."

Me: You'll just say anything, won't you?

 "Apne dil me dard ko jagah de, ilm se shayari nahi aati."

When you'll fall in love with someone someday, you'll understand what I'm going through.

Zubair: I don't want to fall in love with anyone.

Me: Why?

Zubair: *"Jisko bhi dekha rota hua paaya,*
mohabbat toh mujhe kissi fakir ki baddua lagti hai."

Me: …

Zubair: Anjali mentioned you wanted to learn driving.

Me: Yes…

Zubair: Alright! I'll take your driving classes from tomorrow onwards. And please don't say no. This way I'll get to learn some sheero- shaayari as well.

Me: Alright. Bye.

Zubair: Bye.

It was during those driving lessons that I shared my feelings with someone; after a long time.

Never in my wildest dream did I think that Zubair would be the person I'd open up to.

I tried everything to avoid getting this infatuation from turning into love. But my friends did not understand this. Either forcefully or then by making some excuse they would leave me with him. They believed if I spent time with Zubair and stopped thinking about Rayan, I'll be able to move on in life. I tried a lot to move on, if not for myself then for those who loved me so dearly.

I made myself so strong by now, that I decided

I'll put my 100% in trying to make my life and theirs better.

For a week, I deliberated and tried to explain to myself that maybe my friends were right. Maybe Rayan was not in my destiny. Maybe I shouldn't ask Allah for him but rather for his happiness. And maybe Zubair is the angel that Allah had sent to save me. Everyone at my home knew him, my sister loved him, my friends like him… what more did I want?

I was ready to compromise on love. At least everyone would be happy that way.

#13 To new chances

Very few people get a second chance in life and I thought I was amongst those few.

Zubair was my second chance.

I started going out with Zubair, to his parties, meeting his friends. His parents were very nice and I was very close to his sister. Zubair used to call me a magician because I was the only one who could convince his sister to do something, which even his parents couldn't do. Moreover, he felt that I had cast a spell on him. And that was no lie; for I could see his love for me in his eyes. He used to take care of all my needs. He knew that my favourite actor was SRK, so whenever we went for a drive, he'd play his songs. He knew I loved 5 star chocolates. So, whenever we met he gave me a whole lot of chocolates and always sent one for my sister too. He was the first person to send me a message in the morning and the last person to do so at night.

He knew what I wanted before even I realized I needed it. Moreover, he gave it to be before I could even ask for it. So much so that he stopped wearing T shirts when he got to know that I preferred shirts.

Zubair was the dream guy.

It had been 3 months since we started meeting, and by now I knew all his friends. He truly believed that one day or the other, I too would love him the same way he loved me. He bet that such a day would come and I too prayed to Allah asking him for the same. I too wanted to see him the way he saw me. I wanted to make this belief of his come true.

What made him fall in love with me so quickly and with such passion is something I always wondered about. But 'the heart wants what it wants. It knows no time for it and I should know this better than anyone else. Reasons fall short in explaining the matters that concern our hearts.

But I don't know what Allah Ta'la wanted.

Things often aren't as simple as they seem. When I felt that it was time, I could easily move on with Zubair, but it didn't turn out to be that easy.

Meanwhile, my driving classes were still going on. Every morning we went towards India gate and he kept telling me all things I had to know while driving on the way. Then he asked me to try my hand at driving. One fine day, I got down from the car and sat on the driver's seat. I don't know what took over me.

Zubair: What happened?

Me: Nothing. Please drop me home, I don't want to learn.

Zubair: But why? You wanted to learn for so long… What happened?

Me: I don't want to do this anymore. Please, drop me home.

Zubair: If you're scared, I'm there for you.

Me: I'm not scared… I just don't want to learn.

Zubair: What's wrong, Alfisha?

Me: Just take me home. Or else I'll go myself.

Zubair: Okay fine, I'll take you.

I have no clue what happened to me. Why did I act so strangely? I knew very well that it was only for me that he got up so early...and I behaved so badly with him. Why? I don't know myself what I wanted from life.

Zubair did everything to keep me happy, yet I could never bring myself to love him. Why?

Later that evening I got on call with Anjali and Saloni.

Anjali: Do you want to go to Rishikesh tomorrow?

Saloni: I'm in. Who else is going?

Anjali: Our college friends, you, me, Alfisha and Zubair.

Me: Why Zubair? Can't just the 3 of us go?

Anjali: No. I know you guys had a fight. Spend some time together there and you'll feel much better.

Me: Who gives you such ideas?

Saloni: Guilty.

Anjali: Okay guys, so it's a four day trip… and

we'll all have a blast!

Saloni: Count me in on it.

Me: Yes!

Anjali: See you tomorrow then! Bye!

Me: Bye.

Saloni: Bye.

The next morning, I found myself in a car, stuffed between Anjali and Saloni, on our way to Rishikesh. The journey passed with their winks, sly smiles and random one liners.

Rishikesh was a beautiful place; with azure clear sky, water everywhere and peace. The sand, silky under my feel; the breeze, light and fresh. It was nothing like I had experienced in a very long time. I felt like myself a little as I walked along the Ganga. It was this peace, this tranquillity that I was looking for all this while. The change in the air made me change. I could finally think.

All I felt like doing was to sit and stare at the sky the whole day... and I was doing exactly that till Zubair came along.

Zubair: What are you doing all alone over here?

Me: There is so much peace over here… look at the sky… it's so beautiful.

Zubair: Not more than you.

Me: What?

Zubair: Nothing.

Me: I want to ask you something. May I?

Zubair: Sure.

Me: What is it that you see in me? Why do you love me so much? I have only given you tears… still how do you like me so much? You'll get much better girls than me! Then why are so scared of letting me go?

Zubair: *"humne kab manga tumse apni wafao ka silha,*

bas dard dete raha karo, mohabbat jayegi."

Me: What are you trying to tell me Zubair?

Zubair: Nothing. I came to tell you that Amit will be coming tonight and Anjali has made some arrangements for a couple of games.

Me: Okay… Anjali's boyfriend is not coming?

Zubair: No… she's got 4 days of peace, let her enjoy them.

I smiled when I heard that.

Zubair: You look beautiful when you smile.

Me: Thank you.

Zubair: Can you dedicate one sher to me. Please?

Me: *"Kar sako yakeen toh bataoo tumhe,*

bahaut khaas, bahaut khaas, bahaut khaas ho tum!"

I felt as if Zubair was trying to tell me something that day but couldn't. Maybe he was upset with my behaviour. We went to Rishikesh together so we could spend time with each other and get to know each other better, but nothing went as planned. And I take full responsibility for that.

Later, everyone gathered around the bonfire for the games that Anjali had planned.

Anjali: Okay guys, the game goes like this… each one of us can say any dialogue to any person and that person must guess the name of that movie and will also have to complete that dialogue. Has everyone understood?

Amit: Yup! Let's start the game.

Saloni: Amit this is for you-"kaun kambakth

bardaash karne ko peeta hai?"

Amit: "Main to peeta hu ke bass saans le saku," from Devdas.

Anjali: Amit you drink?

Amit: Not at all. It was just a dialogue.

Me: But Saloni does. Right?

Saloni: I DO NOT.

Amit: Are you sure?

Saloni: Yes, Love you too.

Anjali: Saloni, at least listen what he is saying.

Saloni: Haan? Yes, I've had dinner.

Zubair: What is she talking about?

Saloni: ...that I don't drink.

And everyone started laughing.

A minute later, the game began, again.

Zubair: Alfisha this is for you-" Koi pyaar kare toh tumse kare, tum jaise ho waise kare…"

Me: "koi tumhe badalke pyaar kare toh woh pyaar nahi sauda hai," from Bobby.

Anjali: INCORRECT. This is from Mohabbatein.

M : Originally it is from Bobby.

Amit: Yes. She is right.

Saloni: You're all wrong. The dialogue is from Sholey.

Anjali: MOVING ON. Amit, your turn.

Amit: Zubair for you-"Peene ki capacity, jeene ki strength, account ka balance aur naam ka khauf…"

Zubair: "Kabhi bhi kam nahi hona chahiye," from once upon a time in Mumbai.

Me: Uff Allah! What is wrong with you? You guys are just talking about peena pilana .

Zubair : Piyakkad dono!

Saloni: Alfisha for you-"Aaj… aaj ek hasi aur bant lo… aaj ek dua aur maang lo… aaj ek ansoo aur pee lo…?"

Me: "Aaj ek zindagi aur jee lo… aaj ek sapna aur dekhlo… aaj…kya pata kal ho na ho…" from Kal ho na ho.

Anjali: Saloni, don't you know she knows all the dialogues of Shahrukh Khan's movie?

Saloni: Then you guess this one, "Humein to

apno ne loota, gairo mein kahan dum tha…"

Anjali: "Meri kashti bhi doobi wahan, jahan paani kam tha…" from Dilwale.

Me: Zubair for you-"Yaadaashh bhi kitni ajeeb cheez hoti hai… kissi cheez ko puri zindagi bhoolne ki koshish karo, woh bhooli nahi…"

Zubair: "Kabhi ek choti se cheez yaad karne ki koshish karo toh yaad nahi aati," from Jab Tak Hai Jaan. Do you mean it, Alfisha?

Me: …What?

Zubair: What you just said.

Me: No. It's just a game, Zubair.

Anjali: SHUTUP. We are all here together, I'm missing my Nona.

Amit: Nona? What's that?

Saloni: she calls her boyfriend "Nona."

Me: Hehehe…I've heard of "Shona" but never a "Nona."

Amit: Come on, this is in lieu of your name "Yeh jo aap itne bakwaas karti ho, yeh sab free me ya iske paise charge karti ho?"

Saloni: "Nahi nahi, yeh toh free hai…"

Anjali: "Thank God. Kyuki chillar nahi hai mere pass." –Jab We Met.

Me: Good one!

Zubair: One more for you. "Pyaar zindagi ki tarah hota hai, jiska har mod aasan nahi hota, har raste pe khushi nahi milti…"

Me: "Par jab hum zindagi ka saath nahi chhodte, toh hum pyaar karna kyun chhode?"-Mohabbatein

Zubair: Relatable?

Me: ……

Anjali: Alfisha you go now.

Me: "Hum ek baar jeete hai, ek baar marte hai, shaadi bhi ek hi baar hoti hai, aur…"

Zubair: "aur pyaar bhi ek hi baar hota hai,"- Kuch Kuch Hota Hai

Me: Indeed.

Before either one of us could say anything further, Saloni got up and started to look around.

Saloni: Guys, let's eat something.

Amit: yes, I'm feeling hungry.

Me: we'll continue the game later.

As soon as the game ended we got up to leave, but Zubair stopped me and said, "Did you really mean that? Ki pyaar sirf ek baar hota hai…?" I didn't have any answer to give him, so I just laughed off his question. I told him that if he invested so much of his brains in his studies, he'd top his exams. But I think he was very serious… he asked me 2-3 times whether there was something I wanted to tell him. There was something in my heart that I wanted to share with him.

We kept asking each other the same question repeatedly. I don't know why, both of us felt we were hiding something from each other but each of us got the same answer, "Kuch nahi, sab theek hai."

It was our 3rd day in Rishikesh and it was Amit's birthday. We went rafting in the morning and got busy preparing for the celebrations that night. Saloni had put in a lot of effort to prepare everything. They both were the love birds of the group.

We cut the cake at mid night and had a blast…

we danced and sang throughout. Every time I saw Amit and Saloni together, I felt very happy. They both looked at each other so lovingly… that it seemed like they were ready to do anything for each other.

It made me realize that, even today there were some people in this world for whom life is beautiful. They found a way to be with their true love. Every time I got a chance, I told Saloni how lucky she was. And she would always laughingly tell me "Chal pagal… mujhse zyada woh lucky hai." I always thought that love was probably a gift from Allah Ta'la which he gives only to a few lucky people. Saloni was one of them.

That night everyone was singing songs and Amit sang a romantic song for Saloni.

"Baahon ki darmiya… do pyaar mil rahe hai. Jaane kyu bole man, dole sun ke badan, dhadkan bani zuban… Baahon ki darmiya…"

Amit was singing and even danced with Saloni. They looked so beautiful together. After a bit, we left the two of them alone and went to another corner. We were all having food there when suddenly Zubair came there with his guitar and said that he would like to sing for me. Before I could say anything, Anjali said, "Haan haan kyun nahi, zaroor!"

He began singing … "dil ko… tum se pyaar hua… pehli baar hua… tum se pyaar hua… mai bhi, aashiq yaar hua, pehli baar hua, tum se pyaar hua… chhaayi hai betaabi, meri jaan kaho mai kya karu… dil ko… tum se pyaar hua… pehli baar hua… tum se pyaar hua…"

…and it brought everything back.

Me: Stop! Please stop…Stop!!!

Zubair: What happened?

Anjali: What happened? Are you feeling fine?

Me: NOOOO… I'm sorry… I'm not feeling okay… you guys continue.

Anjali: Zubair was singing, at least listen to the whole song before you leave.

Me: No… please … no.

Anjali: But he was singing it for you…

Me: I don't want anyone to sing or do anything for me.

Zubair: Let her go…

Why was I hurting him so much? I wish I could

reciprocate his love. I wish it was all in my hands. But maybe this was impossible. How can I explain that he'd never be happy with me because I'd never be able to love him? Will he understand me? Will he be brave enough to handle it?

People say *"zindagi ustaad se zyada sakth hoti hai. Ustaad sabak dekar imtehaan leti hai aur zindagi imtehaan leke sabak.* I kept wondering how many more times will life test me.

Finally, it was our last day in Rishikesh and the trip turned out to be good for everyone except for Zubair and me. Instead of coming closer to each other, we drifted farther apart.

All of us were busy packing because we had to go for a party that night. While we were busy at this, Zubair stood aloof. His silence and his eyes reflected his agony and he hadn't slept the previous night. This was the first time, I saw someone in such a state because of me. That's why I couldn't understand what I could tell him to bring the smile back on his face. But one thing was for sure; I couldn't lie to him anymore and give him false hopes.

I went up to him and asked him if I could pack for him. Even after repeating it again, when he didn't answer, I packed his bags for him.

At the party, everyone was on the dance floor. Anjali was dancing with her friends and Saloni was with Amit. As always, Zubair and I were left alone. Anjali came over and forced Zubair and me to go on to the dance floor. That day both of us were not in a good mood and all we wanted was to go home. However, Zubair extended his hand to me and said, "One last time please." I couldn't refuse and went with him to the dance floor.

But why did he say "last time"? Was he going somewhere? He had never said something like this!

Everything about that party was so romantic. There was soft music playing, everyone was on the dance floor with their partners. But Zubair and I maintained a distance. I didn't even look at him while dancing. There were tears in his eyes which were telling me a thousand things. I was trying my level best to talk to him, ask him something… but I couldn't get myself to say a single word. It was the first time in my life that I was so scared… I feared Zubair. He was looking at me as if he blamed me for something. His eyes were questioning me and blaming me for spoiling his life. Zubair was also desperate… I had become his weakness. During the dance, my hair kept falling over my face and every time I tried to move it away… it fell back on my face. Zubair came close to me. He had never come this close to me before. He softly pushed my hair behind my ear and he didn't move back this time. I told him twice "Zubair, stay back… I'm not comfortable," but god knows what took over him. He did not seem to understand anything I said. Every time I moved back he came closer to me. I again asked him to take a step back but he didn't listen. Rather he opened my hair. The minute he put his hand on my face, I couldn't hold myself back and slapped him in front of everyone.

The sound of the slap attracted everyone's attention towards us. I didn't have the courage to clarify what happened in front of everyone and so without saying anything I walked away from there. Zubair followed me.

Zubair: Hey stop… please stop. I'm sorry.

Me: Just go from here Zubair. Please go.

Zubair: No. I must tell you something.

Me: What do you think of yourself?

Zubair: Just because someone broke your heart, do you think you can do the same with someone else?

Me: What rubbish are you saying Zubair. Leave me. We'll go home and talk about it.

Zubair: No. We'll talk about it; RIGHT NOW. Can't you see how madly I am in love with you Alfisha? Are you blind?

I have never loved anyone as much as I loved you. I always think of you before myself. Don't you have a heart? What kind of a girl are you?

Me: Let me go, please.

Zubair: You aren't going anywhere. First answer my questions.

And the first thing that came out of my mouth was, "ghabrahaat hoti hai mujhe jab bhi tum mere kareeb aate ho… mera dil mujhe ijazat nahi deta kissi ko kareeb aane ki. Zubair I cannot love you. I tried a lot to forget him but with the passage of time, he kept getting closer to me. I love him profoundly and this love will not change, Zubair. Yes…I don't know whether he too feels the same but it doesn't make an iota of difference to me. I cannot learn to adjust with you, Zubair. Rayan had promised that he would teach me how to drive, how can I give you that place? Tell me? What should I say to you?

Should I ask you to stop playing the guitar? Stop singing the song that Rayaan used to sing for me. "Dil ko tumse pyaar hua" was the song that he used to repeatedly sing for me. I had a right to listen to his song. Only I had rights over his voice. I love my Rayan.

I cannot go with you to watch a movie or to the water park. These were our dreams. We had planned than when he would come to Delhi, we would go to watch a movie and then to the water park. I wanted those dreams to come alive with him. I cannot do it with you, Zubair. Believe me; I have nothing except for these dreams of ours. I'm living only for these dreams of mine and these are all associated with Rayan. PLEASE... let them stay with me.

Zubair, I am not stone hearted. I tried a lot to forget him and fall in love with you... I was determined that I wouldn't break down and wouldn't talk about him anymore. But I've failed Zubair... forgive me. I'm sorry! I tried Zubair....

I really did."

As I wiped tears from my face, I continued.

"You wanted to hear the truth? The truth is that I live a charade. I act at being happy. It is at night, with my misery, my pain, my sorrow and my prayers that I feel close to Rayan. My Rayan.

Yes, I'm dying for him. His is the first and last name in my prayers. He mustn't be doing any such thing for me but that's okay. I can't take revenge for this now, can I? I know that knowingly and unknowingly I have caused you pain. Please find it in your heart to forgive me".

As I looked up I could see Zubair smiling. Before I could question him, he spoke.

"I knew it, Alfisha. I just wanted to hear all that from you. He is a lucky guy. And I pray things work out for you soon."

"Oh, and I'm shifting to London," he added.

"LONDON? When did this happen?"

"I told you it was our last dance!" he replied.

"I will miss you."

"I know."

"Can we be friends again, Zubair?'

"Waapsi ka safar ab mumkin na hoga,
hum toh nikal chuke hai aankh se aasu ki tarha."

"What are your plans for London?"

"Chaand ko dekhunga. Hu- ba- hu tujh jaisa hoga.
Wohi husn, wohi guroor, wohi doori…"

"I'm really sorry, Zubair."

"Tute hue dil se hi shayari nikalti hai, something that I learnt from you."

"Zubair, please forgive me."

"Allah Hafiz, Alfisha."

And to the dusky sky and the dusty roads, I returned my greetings "…. Allah Hafiz!"

Zubair was a beautiful chapter in my life and I was the villain of his life. He danced with his devil, the fallen angel, but I didn't even get that. To this day, I feel bad for how things ended between us.

The truth was someone broke my heart, and I broke his. And I hope Allah could forgive me for that.

To him, I might be the sweet assassin.

For me, he was my saviour.

Who brought Alfisha back.

Epilogue

None of realized that hours had passed.

Umar got up from the bed and with a proud smile said, "So, my little sister has experienced life and love and I was the last one to know?"

"The only one to know," I added.

"Doesn't your Appi know about you little adventure story?" he inquired.

"Nope. No one in the family knows about it. And I'd like to keep it that way," I replied.

"Well...I can't promise that. It is very hard for me to keep a secret from your Appi."

"...Why? You guys hardly talk. And when you do, you always fight. Then how can you not keep a secret from her?" I asked.

"…You're a smart girl. Figure it out, Miss Mature Alfisha"

And then it struck me. Appi and Umar like each other. And not just like, love each other. That is why after every joke they passed each other a sly smile. That is why she always inquired about Umar. That is why she wore a pretty salwar kameez; something Umar always wanted his girl to wear. Like I would have worn that skirt or that frock for Rayan. How could I have been such a fool?

Umar must have understood from my expressions that I have decoded the mystery because he smiled at me and said "You're not the only one who can keep secrets, Alfisha."

I reached out to hug him. I couldn't have been happier.

Appi and Umar were perfect for each other. Two of my pillars of strength had found love. Their love.

Umar brought me to reality when he asked me "So, what is your command for your brother? What should I do to this Rayan of yours? Find him and break his neck?"

I laughed a little.

"…Just pray bhai. Like you have Appi, I hope that someday I'll have him too. And if not him, then I'll be at peace with Allah."

"But today is about you and Appi. I've had just enough of my sob story. Where is she? I need to talk to her. And don't you dare defend your beloved." I added.

He kissed my forehead and took me by the hand and took me to the roof where Appi was star gazing.

The minute I called her out, she laughed and uttered "so you finally know!"

*31ˢᵗ **December 2016***
11:45 pm

Dear Diary,

After a very long time I am feeling happy and satisfied. I am at peace today because I know that my prayers have been answered. I am finally at peace with myself and my decisions.

Unknowingly, Rayan has taught me two

things in life: Patience and believing in the love of Allah.

They say time heals everything. It has the sole power to make you forget everything. This is the rule.

But are two years not enough?

Maybe.

A couple of minutes back, Saloni called and asked me to open my Facebook account. It is really hard to say no to her, so I did as I was asked to do.

As soon as I did that, I saw a message in my Inbox.

Unknown: Hey Alfisha, I want to talk to you about Rayan. It's important.

I was shocked to see this. Who could it be? Is Rayan okay? What does this person want?

So many things went through my mind.

Me(shocked): Who are you?

Unknown : That's not important. Just tell me, are you still in contact with him?

Me: No.

Unknown: Do you still love him?

Me: That is a very personal question.

Unknown: You need to clear the air for me. PLEASE.

Me: Who told you about me?

Unknown: Rayan has told me about you.

Me: Then tell me, who are you?

Unknown: I am his so-called girlfriend. Alfisha, I love him; a lot. And I can do anything to see him happy. But he still loves you. He told me about you from the first day. I believed, with time, I'd seal my place in his heart; but I failed. His heart belongs to you. All of your pictures are still saved in his phone, your gifts are carefully preserved, and he reads your conversation daily and sings your favourite songs.

Me: Are you the same person with whom he had updated a relationship status?

Unknown: Yes. But I updated that status. He rarely uses his Facebook account.

Me: WHY?

Unknown: I am sorry. I am not saying he has not tried to move on with me. He did really. But I guess he can't love anyone else even if he wants to. He remembers everything about you Alfisha.

He blames himself for whatever happened. He just keeps repeating one line day and night. "I have done her wrong. We decided on forever and I just left her." He was, is and always will be madly in love with you.

I couldn't bring myself to reply. Was this really happening. To me? After all this while?

Unknown: There?

Unknown: Hey?

Me: Yes.

Unknown: Please make him happy again. I don't know what to do. I'm in love with him and he is still in a relationship with the memories of you. Everything that I do, every conversation we have; you're there. ALWAYS. I can't take this any longer. If I can't have him, it doesn't mean that you can't.

Me: Hmm.

Unknown: Please, say something. It took me a lot of effort to reach out to you. Do us all a favour and hang in there. For him, for your love. I'm leaving and I'm handing over my Rayan to you. Although he was never mine...Will you take care of him?

Me: Allah ka shukr, I will. Thank you.

I cannot express how happy I am to finally get all my answers.

He still loves me.

Time hasn't healed us. Why would it?

Our pain was the testament how we truly felt.

And what we felt was love; pure and giving. And all-consuming.

As soon as I kept my pen down, I heard my mother calling my name out

"ALFISHAAAAA..."

Before I could reply, she added "You have a call from Kashmir."

<u>Credits for Shayari</u>

1. "Buss ek shaqs mere dill ki zidd hai,
   na uss jaisa chahiye,   na uske siwa chahiye."
                                        - NIMRA YASMEEN

2. "Iska gham nahi tha ki 'usne' bardaad kiya,
   ghum iska tha k, bahut der k baad kiya.
                                        - MASROOR ANWAR

3. " Ye mujhe chain kyu nahi parta,
   ek hi shaks tha jahaan me kya."
                                        -JOHN ELIA

4. "Mai aur usko bhula du?
   kaisi baate karti hai yaar,
   surat toh fir surat hai,
   wo naam bhi pyara lagta hai"
                                        - FARAZ

5. "Woh bewafaa hargis na tha, yon hi badnam hogaya.
   hazaro chane wale the, kis kis se wafa karta"
                                        - FARAZ

6. "Uski bewafai par fida hote hai is kadar jaan tere,
   khuda jaane agar usne wafa ki hote toh tera kya hota."
                                        - FARAZ

7. "Khairaat mai mili khushi mujhe acchi nahi lagti,
   mai apne dukhon mai rehti hu nawaabon ki tarah."
                                        - FARAZ

ACKNOWLEDGEMENT

'WITH THE FAITH I HAVE IN YOU ALLAH! ,

In the process of putting this book together, I realised how true this gift of writing is for me.

To Mom and Dad, thanks for understanding the things I said, The things I didn't say and The things I never planned on Telling you.
You 'll be with me like a handprint on my heart.

To my sister, Zulfitaha: who told me not to give up on my dreams and that everything that's good takes time.
I guess now is the time for good!

To my Best friends, Anjali and Tanya : you guys have given me the most support when you didn't realise that I needed it. That's the most. Thank you for your jokes when I was down on myself, got me over a great many humps.

To My support system,
Sajid: you reckoned my creativity through our many conversations and kick it sessions.
Thank you for not just believing, but knowing that I could do this.

I had no idea, I would be publishing a book, but you all confided in my efforts without knowing where I would lead.
Thanks for our visits, our talks and our closeness.
Much love to you guys.

ABOUT THE AUTHOR

Nida Ahmed is a young enthusiast studying English Literature from Hindu College, University of Delhi. She's passionate about her aims, fully alive, confident, and outdoorsy.

She through her first novel portrays that very person who's given away their everything and never sought anything but love.

Let's find out what she has in store for all.